I0726923

CENTRAL:
THE CELTIC PRIESTHOOD OF
Samhain

Illustrated By: Inez Sanders

Michael L. Watts Jr.

This publication contains the opinions and ideas of its author. It is intended to provide helpful and informative material on the subjects addressed in the publication. The author and publisher specifically disclaim all responsibility for any liability, loss or risk, personal or otherwise, which is incurred as a consequence, directly or indirectly, of the use and application of any of the contents of this book.

WORKBOOK PRESS LLC
187 E Warm Springs Rd,
Suite B285, Las Vegas, NV 89119, USA

Website: https://workbookpress.com/
Hotline: 1-888-818-4856
Email: admin@workbookpress.com

Ordering Information:
Quantity sales. Special discounts are available on quantity purchases by corporations, associations, and others. For details, contact the publisher at the address above.

Library of Congress Control Number:
ISBN-13:   978-1-958176-87-0 (Paperback Version)
                978-1-958176-88-7 (Digital Version)

REV. DATE: 07/06/2022

CENTRAL:
The Celtic Priesthood of
Samhain

Michael L. Watts Jr.

Central: The Celtic Priesthood of Samhain

"We just received a report of a public disturbance, what should we do sir?" The Constable said.

"Have a team go check it out," Constable Greg responded.

"I could sir, but we sent out fifteen men and they've… I think we need the whole squad sir." The Constable stated.

"The whole squadron!" Constable Greg exclaimed.

"Sir, Sir!" The second Constable cried. "We just captured a group of four vigilantes that almost demolished half the staff."

"Now, let me see who's in charge," says Constable Greg.

The man led the group to the cell were the captives laid motionless. The Constable had informed the chief that they fought for quite some time and that it took the help of military personal to bring them in.

"The fight that he led was something that was unheard of sir, there were so many bodies out there in the streets that I think we have lost count." The Constable grimly stated.

"Let me see whoever it is in charge!!" Constable Greg demanded.

The group of Constables escorted the Chief Constable to the cells where the group of people were being held. Within that grouping they had noticed that three of them looked as if they couldn't have been but around the age of twenty or so. The chief Constable immediately insinuated that the three couldn't have been the leader yet he stormed in asking questions.

"You young lady, how old are you?" Constable Greg asked.

"I'm twenty one." The lady answered.

"Okay then, who is in charge over here?" Constable Greg asked.

The older woman was brushed up against the cell wall, pulling the hair from her eyes and brushing it to the back of her head. She was hesitant to answer any questions. The two other teens males began to look among each other in frustration. What should they do, should they began telling the Constable what's at stake or just stay quiet?

"Hey I'm talking to all of you, I said who is in charge?" Constable Greg asked again more firmly.

The older woman picked herself up from the cell wall before she began to speak. A great fear rippled through the cell and the four fighters were pressed with its aura.

"I am." The woman answered.

"Great then, you're the one that I want to interrogate. Get her out of this cell." Constable Greg demanded.

The guards took action in restraining the woman and

preparing her for the interrogation room. She was cuffed with a pair of chained wrist locks that warped her wrist as the hard tight metal clamped against her skin.

"Chief Constable Greg, the woman is restrained." The guard said.

"Continue onward to the interrogation room." Constable Greg demanded.

A few winding halls and they ended up to another room that held nothing but a desk and two chairs that said interrogation on the outside door. From there the woman sat until Constable Greg returned to proceed with his interrogation. In the distance she could hear the two men speaking with one another about the fight outside of the police station.

"Madam, my name is Constable Greg. Are you aware of why I have detained you?" Sasha remained silent at the just of Constable Greg's questioning. "So has anyone come forth to suggest what happened or who started the brutal fight?" Constable Greg asked.

"No sir, nobody was either alive or even available in the area to witness anything." The guard responded.

The door opened and then Constable Greg enters into the interrogation room with a quick eye set on the woman. He places a cup onto the table and then asked the woman if she was thirsty, reluctantly she declined.

"So who are you and your group of individuals? Why have you come to my city?" Constable Greg asked.

The woman let out a quick sigh and then began giving into the Chief's questions. Her timing was imminent if she wanted to make a point about how they were subjected to the grounds in the first place.

"My name is Sasha alongside of Buckner, Cash, and Sicily. We came here to take shelter at the temple and begin studies of the Celtic Priesthood. The group of thugs that we fought…" She said.

"Excuse me, those thugs were part military and police officials." Constable Greg said.

"Sure to the standards that you understand, as far as I know it they were no good lives who answer to a power that is greater than you or any other force alive." Sasha stated.

"Is that right? Do you care to explain this to me?" Constable Greg insisted.

Sasha was quiet, she didn't want to create a panic that was beyond her current authority. For any other matter she knew that she would come off as a crazy lady who only sought to do her worst in crime. But she also thought on one hand, why not? Why not unleash an untold truth that would be a possible barrier of either life or death.

"So it begins like this; the history that has been outside of your understanding for so many years…" She said.

"The priesthood is at an all-time high reign of power but has fallen short during the turn of governance. The church has become a second hand source of power in comparison to those that have ruled or left the world afar. The priesthood had become overthrown and began to falter until a single soul had turned the hands of faith, hail the lord Samhain."

"What does this priesthood have to do with anything that is of importance to me or the group of dead individuals within the streets?" Constable Greg asks.

"The priesthood has to do with everything that is physical in this world Constable Greg," Sasha stated confidently.

"The temple guards had been on watch towards the unity of the church. Inside the Priesthood they continued to praise and worship in prayer and sacrifices of horse and humans alike. Harmony had contained the grounds of the Celtics priest and nothing could be disclosed that would fray the beliefs alike. The fallen shadows are those that have contained the unrighteous acts of the priesthood for God."

"Sacrifices! What sacrifices are you talking about?" Constable Greg insisted.

~~~

"Though to the ideal prospect of the priesthood they had only followed the works of the Lord. The temple Sanctuary were decorative of the same insights as Moses described in the nature of the bible; fine twined linen, blue, purple, and scarlet. Golden
~~~

candle sticks made with six branches, an altar of smitten wood. All executed of an exact design. The priesthood was only some of the most loyal of subjects to God by the name of Jesus.

They once held accounts of the son and father and the belief of reality. With this held the swallow of the dead spirits that swarmed in against life. To them all were true because of the life that was constructed by the Father, and the acts that were condoned. Life was an alarming blend of belief and disbelief of the actuality that it is and the priesthood had known what was to become of it.

The reason of faith had only concluded itself by the priest scholars who lectured to the upcoming youth. The children of the Priesthood women and men alike all aged beneath twenty years of living. All open to the hands of idealism, all open to the cause of destruction. Inside of the sanctuary the fine twined linens hung from pillars that engulfed the room. Restively the children listened in the consumption of the lectures by the elders."

"Lectures, please explain this." Constable Greg said. "What does this have to do with the wild fight."

"Soon you will understand my lord." Sasha said.

"Even after the hands of sorcery one must become one with the father, the truest friend of all." The Celtic priest Samhain said to his crowd of youthful priest.

"Without the help of the Father, then coercive things almost become destructive in a punitive fashion. An outcast of what reality is and what designs where sub-commanded to the priesthood's creative hands of obstruction to life," the priest finished saying.

A room of fifteen teens, six were dark skinned of multiple nationalities and the other nine were white Europeans, and all sat Indian style in admiration of the elder priest. The day was an opposite day of their combative training. It was a day which started the week's lessons of sorcery and witchcraft. There were students that were not receptive to the accounts of the lessons, though Samhain was even in his conduction of the lessons.

"So with what has been said, let us not refute the main course of today's lessons, because they may become your last mean of survival." Samhain said.

He raised his hand and began to channel energy through his palm. With his hand high in the air he said, "Take the energy…"

He brought his hand back down toward his natural line of vision and tight-fisted his palm. A confirmed sighting of a yellowish field channeled around his hand and ignited the minds of the young scholars. A select few of the fifteen rose and stood to get a better view of the sight. A wondrous awe had filled the crowd of young scholars.

"Then you control the plane of direction, thus making a containment spell. Something this simple takes energy, alone it would be difficult to harness and fight at the same time, but together it's a powerful touch," Samhain continued.

One of the standing children awed and began to approach Samhain. His small body frame froze on the approach, keeping him away at a distance. The scholar's eyes roamed to see the frozen peer looking at the masterful craft of the elder priest. Samhain's control had reigned once again among the peers. Behind his glasses the boy's eyes had veered from left to right and below him.

"This power is something that you must will it to gather its strength, it's something that you beg of the father. Surely his will is well forgiving for miss direction of death and self-control. The energy makes its appearance for the mistakes of death and self-control is all that we are." Samhain concluded.

The frozen boy muffled a loud distress call released in his captivity. Samhain hones in on the unwoven child, in an attempt to subdue him.

"Remembering this lesson could be life or death to the young approaching student. Remember what is volatile in the forth coming race of what life really is to become because even in your oldest age redemption isn't so often given by luck." Samhain said to the on-looking peers.

None of them said a word. They only looked onward in disbelief of what to recall. How to become a great sorcerer priest like Samhain at his best?

"Sir," the younger looking female said in astonishment, "will you release Buckner?"

The boy with the glasses still stood silently without any

bodily movement. His name was Buckner, one of the few scholars who were able to deliver on the outlandish demands of Samhain. He was one that was top of the class and yet very optimistic of demands.

"Of course I am Sicily." Samhain responded.

He removed his hand from Buckner's direction, therefore releasing the energy field held against his smaller body frame, giving him freedom. The boy shifted his weight from left to right in disbelief. His eyes swept toward his hands as he watched his movement in speculation. A cheery smile rose to the boy's face as he tried the same containment spell against Samhain. Again the boy had frozen.

"Sorcery is at the least fantasy ma'am and not real." Constable Greg said.

"Oh but it is sir, it truly is," Sasha stated.

During the casting of his spell, Samhain's body glowed with a bright and shiny green color that illuminated him. The scholars awed again at the priest's superior ability. Buckner on the other hand was frozen within an entranced stupor.

"What had happened?" Sicily yelled out in fear for Buckner. "Why hasn't he moved again?"

The group of scholars all watched Buckner in his attempts to escape the immeasurable enchantment. Seamlessly enough as it should be, he couldn't. Instead he was frozen with a full smile upon his face as if he was a mime.

"Don't be alarmed," Samhain soothingly said, "I only reflected his magic…," Samhain stopped speaking.

Immediately he released his reflection spell and submitted to Buckner's own containment spell. The group of teens marveled at the spectacle. It was never before seen to them the submissiveness of Samhain until now. Buckner had been noted by classes of mages as first in his class. The smile that Buckner wore had widened as a glow of bright yellow color emitted from his fist, still facing the uncanny Samhain. Buckner was one of the best even though he displayed a form to gravel after the priests. The young group had become stumped for words.

He opened his palm and released the same clutches that Samhain had once had on him. A gasp had filled everyone's ears as they prepared for Samhain's counter spell.

"And that is a proper spell being cast. Buckner I'll need to talk to you after the class is over." Samhain said to the young priest.

Everyone in session was still in amazement as to how Samhain the great sorcerer lord could be had by a student. They all were impressed. Everyone was impressed except for Buckner. Even Sicily, the frail red head who cared for him in their years past was grateful to have such a close relationship with the scholar.

"We practice together. Really whenever we can get the chance to," she said.

Buckner only gave a short reverence of a smile that he folded shortly after. He realized that his success in another task was a bit more than what anyone else had expected.

"Is there anyone else that is able to produce the containment spell? Please try now or forever cheer for peace," Samhain proclaimed.

The scholars had grown quiet with no chance of dispute. Oddly they mostly feared the laughter that would only take place for not getting the spell right. Only the most stern and courageous scholars were more able to have ease with the spell, scholars like Cash. Cash was mostly named second of mages in comparison to Buckner. Eventually the second to succeed was the limit that was drawn about him. He was never a full-fledged leader, but he mustered enough courage to at least be successful.

Cash's energy drew to him quickly as he stood with the same yellow glow aimed from his hand. He flashed the glowing hand around the court, over all the scholars to his right as he clamped down on his palms, creating a fist. There was a silhouette action that could have overthrown any handful of unsuspecting people. The section of scholars all had been contained. Sweat beads ran from his brow and he shook convulsively.

"So these youths know magic, how am I to believe that?" Constable Greg asked.

"Just believe sir," Sasha said.

She continued with her story. She didn't want to disturb

what she was getting at with her story nor did she want to disturb the peace that the Constable had for himself in not knowing.

"See, it's not about what you do with the power, not at all. It's more toward how much of the power that is being used. Scholars please pay attention." Samhain said modestly. "If you can, continue to hold the containment, Cash."

Cash followed with Samhain's order even though he already wanted to release the hold. He was driven to unease at the thought. Tiring from the hold of the spell, Cash fell to one knee with his fist still drawn. The young man's eyes flickered in a fast flutter drawing him to a thunderous fall, he collapsed. The section of scholars held by his containment spell were released from the containment as they all turned their focus onto Cash.

"Cash, Cash!" Sicily stuttered, 'Sir he's not responding.'

"I know," Samhain replied calmly, "His would only lead to another spell, it is the Resurrectional…"

~ ~ ~

"So do you really expect me to believe this as a true story?" Constable Greg asked.

"Look." Sasha said devilishly.

This is it so listen clearly. There is a history for what has gone and this is all that I actually know so pay close attention."

The cold wind brought in by the shadowing of the sun had

a familiar draw. A chill blew from the dam with an uneasy feeling that would only appear and reappear at the coming of the full moon. The silent night had its own fill of those things that creeps around. A set of howls carries itself among the silent winds that blow in a grateful ease. Somewhere past the city limits border, a battle has started.

An arid group of vampires distinct in their difference in clans, also named blood suckers have taken a fight against the more violent feral dogs called werewolves. For centuries the two clans have fought unnoticed by the sights of average onlookers, unless they were being charmed or maimed. Enchanted to be taken in and used as the next of kin in rally or by form. Each side has taken helpless wanderers to be of aid in battle.

Swooshing and soaring sounds floated on the winds and sands as the vampires hovered above the race of wolves, by them who had followed upon foot. Snarling and barking they each took attempts at biting a flying vampire. Within the reach of the wolf only to come short by the foot as they fevered for the blood of the vampires. Lucky, a large gray colored female wolf, took the initiative to attack. A row of leafless trees stood far ahead of her that she used to pounce up the branches consecutively before leaping for another blood sucker.

"Wait, do you really expect me to believe that this has something to do with wolves and vampires? My lady it is insane to believe in such a hoax. It's a fairy tale to tell children to keep them in line." Constable Greg recited.

"Please just listen to the history of my story if you want answers." Sasha insisted.

"Give me a second." Constable Greg said. He excused himself from the interrogation room and made his way to a fellow Constable where he insisted that they be on extreme watch. It seemed that the story was making a grave detail of a delusion that he knew was of no good.

"Please continue onward with this, extreme case of emergency," he said as he sat down.

The attempt was all without gratification as the beast fell harshly toward the ground in a swift motion that left a dent in the dirt. Her sharp snarling teeth had released the vampire that she held onto as she had to catch a second breath. The wounded vampire glided away from Lucky in the hopes of an escape though it was caught off guard by another prowling wolf. The wolf who tried to pounce on top of the abrasive vampire had missed as the vampire had barrel rolled around the beast in its flight. Free from the second wolf the vampire ascended back into the air and away from the dogs.

The pack had ran ahead of Lucky who trailed only a few feet behind. They continued running faster and stronger than they ever had before, continuing on the vampires trail. With enough power the leading wolf had attempted the same climbing of trees as lucky had done. Only this attempt was the one to take down a blood sucker by the wolf pack. The wolf sprung high and captured the last vampire, swinging him with its sharp teeth and tossing him to the ground. The scent of blood propelled the eagerness of the wolves as the pack rushed the downed vampire, all of them shredding its flesh. The vampire cried out as his flock swarmed away from the fight. The cry could be overheard by the howling of the wolves who had gotten their fill from the flesh of the blood suckers. Upset at the lacking of an onslaught they prepared for the return to their lair just past the woods.

~

It didn't take Samhain too long to teach the group of young scholars how to deliver the reincarnation spell and the restoration spells. They had begun to get overwhelmed by the casting of the restoration spell in which select few would claim that they had begun feeling better than what they had before the spells were cast. A few others would rectify the statement by stating that nothing was actually happening to them and that the novices weren't ready for the overloading spell.

"I should reconcile the ideas that anything has occurred or not. The spells are meant for regeneration of a loss of energy and it may call for lots of favor with the father. The will that is the underlying source of energy add a balance of control," Samhain implied.

"But sir we aren't even ready for that yet," Cash said.

"Cash..." Sicily muffled, "he's still weak from the containment."

"Oh please do tell." Constable Greg said while pulling out

a notepad to write on.

"That's because the will of your young hearts have not been fully forgiven by the father. Otherwise you would have found out how to control the energy that it takes to harness the power for regain and reincarnation," Samhain said.

The group of scholars had become saddened by the news and they were petrified as to how and why couldn't they reach out to the father.

"When will we be forgiven?" A scholar cried out.

"Yeah," the group cried out.

The class was in awe that morning, yet they were left to believe that they haven't been forgiven by the father for a lack of will and spirit. The retribution, of an inclination that caused them to feel sorrowful to their punishment from God that they have been handed. Silence had overtaken the group until Buckner again petitioned about the strength of his abilities.

"May I sir?" he asked of Samhain.

Samhain was without question as he urged the young scholar to continue with the process of casting the regain spell. The scholar began by raising both of his hands into the air with all fingers fully spread. His hands were aimed over Cash's body as he lay helpless with little energy with his face in the ground. Buckner shook and strained while clutching his teeth hard and moaning viciously. A red glow came atop his hands and over the body of

Cash.

"Again I marvel at your ambition young scholar!" Samhain replied in exclamation to what Buckner was doing. "A second action should take place and that is when the deed is finished."

The group of scholars took watch of Buckner's display of regain over Cash's body. It wasn't long before both scholars glow had changed colors from red to a white flash before fading to a green color.

"When it is finished, is when the two bodies would give regain back to one another in a reflexive action of regeneration." Samhain said while displaying a brisk smile of cheer. "It is great to see my best scholars progressing so well."

"Sir," The warrior priest Nattuck called to Samhain.

"Nattuck," Samhain replied to the dark priest.

"I'm surprised to see you this early on your return from your journey. Was everything as we have expected?"

Nattuck took a few of steps toward Samhain. It's been over three months since the two have seen each other and for a great reason. Nattuck had taken a journey of skill through the dark forest alongside of Maxin and Elee. Usually when a priest has finished the lessons of the scholars they take the Journey. It's a trial of a dangerous pursuit of the beast of the woods; against the feral dogs. Not too many were able to take the journey and live to tell about it though Samhain was the first in this accomplishment.

"Everything came to a standstill Sir with Elee and Maxin," Nattuck claimed.

"He's alright I am sure." Samhain concluded.

Nattuck took a closer step toward Samhain, drawing closer toward his left ear. He began to whisper to him.

"The matter is more urgent than anything else and it could be life or death Sir. We believe Maxin has been poisoned sir. He is very ill and unresponsive to us." Nattuck said.

Samhain stopped speaking and drew closer toward his group of scholars. He gave them a feverish look before he begun to protest to them. His eyes had widened and his attitude had changed to a more sovereign state than a teacher's would.

"Today is finished and Buckner I will continue with you later and as for the rest of the class we will regroup tomorrow for combative courses. Please help Cash up as I must go. Everyone is dismissed," He said.

Following Nattuck's lead, Samhain turned and followed the younger priest to the medical wing of the sanctuary. The path drove them back east through the temple and past a sectioning of other rooms. On the far side of the temple was the wing where they found Maxin being watched over by Elee the Earth Priestess.

"Sir." Elee addressed him as she approached the two Priests and grabbing Samhain's hand. "He's not alright and we don't know why."

The three had all walked back to Maxin's location, where he was propped up on a mat. Elee took the time to kneel back by his side to place a warm cloth upon his forehead. She then held onto his hand that lay near her; pulling it to her chest.

"Maxin please, my heart is racing for you to recover. Samhain your lord is here, please speak to us!"

Samhain knelt down to feel for Maxin's pulse that showed a faint sign of life. Beat after beat the pulse thumped in his hand.

"How long has he been like this?" Samhain asked

"Close to a week." Nattuck responded.

Samhain stood, standing behind the trio with his arms crossed. His own instinct at that point had become gentle to take action. Nattuck watched the priest intently.

"He shows signs of life but he's not responsive, but how can this be?" Samhain incurred.

"We do not know Sir! We had hoped that you would be able to tell us this by your own words," Nattuck said.

"Is that so?" Samhain said while rubbing his chin.

Samhain opened Maxin's eyes with two of his fingers. He looked at the pupils of the colleague to see how he has been affected and if he could spot any signs. The cornea had gone bloodshot and filled with moisture. The priest's mouth was very moist and warm to the touch. His saliva glands had been inflamed with thickness.

"He shows no real imperfections other than his bloodshot eyes and his thickened saliva. Are there any scars upon him?" Samhain ask.

Nattuck and Elee had taken a glance at one another then back toward Samhain. The both of them had an expression on their face that exaggerated the loss to the question.

"We checked," Elee said, "and…"

"Nothing," Nattuck intervened. "Not even a scratch."

"You faced two months on the journey and no wounds are apparent and this has happened to Maxin. So could you tell me what happened once you reached the dark forest?" Samhain questioned.

"Sure, but…" Nattuck began.

"It will not be easy," Elee finished.

She began to describe the terrain of the grassy dark forest and how vivid it was in color and sharpness of trees. With much to say that it favored a jungle, Samhain knowing the interloping insects didn't question an infestation. The description had consumed him when Elee described the flooring as a graveyard of human remains of bones. Ribs, femur, and skulls all lay to waste by some force of terror in the area.

"We became alarmed," Nattuck said. "But we didn't want to quit the journey."

"Then what happened?" Samhain asked.

Nattuck's explanation didn't come easy, saying that they traveled onward before they had reached a cave. From inside the cave a rumbling could be heard, distorted but loud noises.

Samhain's keen listening skills came to his aid at the settling of the next night. He followed the paths that had been described to him without any fear in mind just the pure faith that something may conclude to the state of Maxin. He had to humble himself in taking on this task by himself, without any source of an extended hand. Anybody else would have trembled at the thought yet Samhain was different as evident of how he's in a search for peace. Elee voice raced through his mind as she finished the story of her three month journey of life in the wild.

"The rumbling was weird almost satanic," Elee said.

"We thought that it could have been a ritual and we were right." Nattuck followed to say. "A glare came from inside of the cave as if it was a distant fire. Shadows were cast on the walls, the people that were inside all where dancing in a high praise. They were all excited about something."

"They danced around the fire chanting, *"amongst us they will raise at the eve of the LAST DAY."* Elee stated.

Samhain continued on his path without double tracking

his place to match what he remembered in detail. The conversation of the detail spoken words were racing fast within his mind as he stepped closer to what he believed to be the cave she spoke of.

"We don't know what it meant, but it sounded serious." Elee continued.

"Was that the last of it?" Samhain asked

"Actually, no," Nattuck recalls. "It wasn't."

"We edged our way through the inside to get a better glance and then we came to an alarming halt." Elee stated.

"We were spotted, forcing us to fight. We held a strong battle with the better use of Elee's Earth magic she cast a haze throughout the cave and even though fire began to swarm us." Nattuck followed.

"Closely we weren't burned and we retreated, though Maxin was out of sight away from me and Nattuck's reach."

"That was when the battle had broken outside of the cave and I lost my bow somewhere. Luckily I drew my sword and protected us. Elee's quick thinking used her cast and containment spell and allowed me to slay the men. We were safe again, but we still couldn't find Maxin."

"Well where did you find him?" Samhain asked encouragingly.

Elee looked for Nattuck to finish the story that had

Samhain readily sitting closer to them. He reached his hands out to touch the both of them, patting their shoulders while tilting his head downward.

"It's alright I understand. It is too difficult to say'" Samhain said.

"The exact opposite Sir, Maxin was still in the cave, yet a priest of some sort who was dressed in black had taken a hold of him. By then we could only tell that he was being forced to drink something, it looked like blood!!" Nattuck finished.

Samhain slowly lifted his head upward and faced Nattuck, he became discouraged by his words. A slit came to his eyes as they dropped and he turned to face Maxin.

"We stopped the man though he got away through another passage beyond the caves walls."

Samhain was taken aback and wanted retribution for one of his top scholars whom he began to call brethren. But what was exactly within his will of duty to debug what he began building for people to understand. Don't under estimate the power of the will of God, and to do so that meant being obedient to those that also follow.

That night prior to Samhain leaving he asked Elee and Nattuck to watch over the scholars and to continue with the combative lessons for the day. He was going to journey to reach what was evident about the cave that they were in. If anything important was to be found then it would be there, waiting in a hidden space. Surely he knew something could be done and that it was about the time and fashion to have it done. The travel was a half a day's travel if on horseback, a route that he knew too well.

The off settled black forest was outside of the cities walls, miles of wild terrain. The forest was close to the smaller city of Idel that lay at the bottom of the rivers drop off. Samhain had sought the cave and was able to examine it in full aspect, yet the blood that was shed had left a stench that agitated his nostrils. The ungodly sight was just as horrific and offensive, the cave was hollow and void of any active life other than the bones around him.

Nothing stood out as a resonating clue to who the cloaked individual was or where they had gone, though Samhain was already prepared for the account. He managed to learn a spell during his years of practice that can reach a mind and adoptively see last perceptions and possible futures. After the greater establishment of his skill he failed to reveal the skill to his peers, a thought that had haunted him this day. He chanted as he reached one of the minds of the dead men of the cave and he witnessed everything.

The cloaked pale man had forced the drink on Maxin with brute force of pressure to Maxin's throat. It was the last sight before Samhain began exploring the man's visions that had informed Samhain about the war with the Vampires. The same sight that embellished the return of the hunting packs during the late night hours. This time that was relatively concurrent and shaped the future of Samhain's direction of thought. Samhain had seen what he needed to know and what to do further.

He began to step onward through the cave before loud howls had thrown him off guard. He hadn't come in contact with a wolf in years and he didn't want to mark the account just yet. At the end of the cave were a few cracks and one was large enough to fit an adult body through. The priest made his move through the small crawl space feet first. He wanted to be able to land on his feet at the chance of an uncharted fall. Samhain had prolonged his descent in a hope to be able to eavesdrop on the wolves.

At the approach they began to howl a more terrifying shriek. The shrill sounds echoed loudly in the caves hollowness. Samhain's ears ring with pain, thus throbbing against the loud shrilled howls that echoed within the caves walls. He still held on to keep a close eye on what was to take place. He noticed the pack of wolves all surrounding the dead pack members.

Some of the wolves whimpered as they began crying indiscreetly, the larger gray wolf named Lucky had shifted back to her human form, dropping down to her knees. She whaled even louder in distress.

"No, but how? Why?" She gestured. "We worked too hard to get this large and we fall short once again. Who ever done this will pay by the hands of the pack until our end had succeeded. Search the area, come back with any clues."

A handful of the wolves had left the cave in a hunt for any living sources. Samhain was silent during the scavenging. Any abrupt sound would have sent him to his next rest as supper.

"We were coming so much closer to ridding this world of those vampires and now they are hunting us." Lucky continued.

Samhain had to think if he had ever met a vampire before, a thought that he could never recall. Time upon time their priests have spoken about the claims of the creatures terracing life as he knew it. It wasn't until now that he concluded to accept the thoughts of the laddish creatures. He began understanding that he was out of place in aspects of what to think about the new information. A cloaked man had tortured one of his pupil priests and he didn't expect the wolves to give him a clue.

He realized that he had done just that and the same. The wolf pack leader Lucky continued rumbling on about how they had planned to rule the world as the only walking creatures to life. This statement he began fumbling through his mind in a fog. The Journey wasn't without cause as he reminisced the importance of the priesthoods training. He hoped the strenuous effort of his lectures wouldn't have to be done so in vain.

He only imagined the need to use his skills for fighting, something indefinite would only follow this day to him. Strangely enough he caught eye of a wolf that was sniffing smells quite long and closed to crevice that held Samhain. Was he onto Samhain? Had he conjured a scent of a possible rodent laid for torment? Samhain drew less to either thought and only to the prized get away.

Only being clueless to a full understanding Samhain was ready to make his move. At a sudden the wolf disappeared from sight to only have crept to the opening of the hole. The large fangs of the beast hurled its open jaws in hopes of engulfing him with his teeth, the body of Samhain. The beast was so startling that Samhain yelled in terror. The priest released his grip alongside of the tunnels walls, descending through the crack.

Within its perceived ability the wolf had followed and gotten its hind legs caught in the entrance. It snapped ferociously at Samhain's face that was in close range to its teeth.

"Oh no," Samhain stammered and feared his death to come.

Even if he had wished to move he couldn't have done so as easily. He had a satchel bag that was pressing against a rock in the tunnel and it kept him at bay, Rubble tumbled down the tunnel that had chipped from the wolf's body pressed against the rock. It seemed that he was slowly inching his way through the tunnel and Samhain was stuck. The smell of blood hovered from the wolf and Samhain knew he was next.

It was clear that he had to get rid of the satchel, but it wasn't his preferred option. The satchel had a set of orbs that were used to channel his spells at a higher rate of energy then he could ever master. He couldn't dare lose track of them or it would become hazardous for him to use high grade spells. At this point the choice was becoming way too much for him to handle. With at least one orb in his possession he could battle his way to the rest.

Samhain thought fast when he removed the strap from his shoulder. After doing so he managed to grab one orb from the sack.

To his discontent the wolf was on a steady approach, squeezing through the tunnel. It took another snap that caused Samhain to jump and release himself from the rock. He was free to shimmy himself further down the tunnel as he did. Down another foot was all he could go because of the fall off that cliff was hidden from his sight.

Nothing, but adrenaline kept Samhain steady to be able to attempt what he did next. He began focusing on the beast, glowing an orange array around him he chanted.

"From the beginning to the end, what has started will submit to an end."

A white aura came over him and flushed throughout the cave, and immediately the wolf before him began to slide further into the tunnel. Snapping and snarling his monstrous fangs, Samhain drew further down the tunnel in relation to the speed of the wolf until he could move no more. Samhain drove himself to the edge where he hung with one hand on the rocky ledge and an orb in the other. The wolf had stopped face to face with Samhain yet not in the form of a wolf but that of a human.

"What have you done to me?" The man asked.

"I gave you back humanity," Samhain replied. "Something that you've longed needed."

The man was confused though enraged with what had happened. He was human but not by his own will or by the manifest of sunset. It was the magic of God's doing and he wasn't at all happy by it. The man began to despise Samhain deeply.

"For that you will pay," The man said.

The man hung with his feet latched to the same rock that had captured Samhain. He reached outward to take a swing at Samhain with his fist. Except, the movement of Samhain was way too swift to catch for the halfhearted man as he sway away from the approaching fist. The smell of salt water had already informed Samhain about his descent through the cave. It leads to a water tap that headed to some sort of runoff. Now or never was his thought as he released his grip to the ledge as his better choice over death.

The coming of the darkened night sky was brewing rage within the cave of the wolf pack. The humane walkers were speechless to the action that had overcome and changed him. With no other understanding Lucky was astonished at the transition. Something that easily done could be undone, if by will alone. A new power had surfaced and it was coming to Lucky to be able to harness it.

~~~

Morning had come too early for Elee and she wanted a chance to rest this morning. Though she knew she couldn't due to the short hand of priest within the synagogues. One thing was certain was that the children were awaiting more training and Elee was the best fit. She was a strong swordsman but an even better archer. On top of her physical combative skills she was an even better sorceress of magic, especially with sand and earth.
~~~

Against the ranks of her colleagues, Nattuck and Maxin, she was worthy of being labeled a top priestess. She excelled and exceeded them all by being open to the lessons and giving back even more from understanding. Revolution had clued her to her devotion to the priesthood for a time like this. The time would come that she would lead behind Samhain as the next in charge. It was a dream of goals that she had founded while young in age when she realized how she loved Samhain.

Samhain was the first man to ever cast her to a state of calm, which drove her passionately. Never had she expressed her feelings to anyone other than Samhain himself. She rebelled at his compassion for the priesthood over her. She believed he was crazy to carry a dream without involving any passion for a woman. At the same she was driven to prove her worth to him and the priesthood.

Getting up before the children could was of major importance to the priesthood. It nourished a balance of good control, maturity and seniority. All of these were qualities that she managed all too well. For her given chance of leadership she wanted it to be perfect. Elee wanted to show the younger scholars that she was a prime element of authority and knowledge. Her preparations for the courses were underway after she'd tended to her hygiene.

Being a priestess Elee examined one of the highest qualities of excellent hygiene even after exertive workouts. Her bathing was lustrated, with milk and honey with jasmine rose pedals to heighten her elegant scent that redefined her charm. The process was a heavy form of rejuvenation for her that medicates well. Now she was ready to put together the structural lessons to drive the peers' skill to a high. Hand to hand combat was one of her favorite skills over any.

Elee began setting the equipment for the scholars to train with, wooden swords that can sting like a horde of bees in the summer. Evenly she set the weapons across from one another to indicate the stream of partners for each scholar. Her layout was well planned since she knew that the class was uneven and that she would have to spar with a scholar. Alone she couldn't imagine a better lesson plan for the young group. It was time that they knew how to become graceful with a sword and she was the best teacher.

Ahead of schedule, it was time for the students to begin breakfast, yet she meditated in preparation. Her position was being marked and tested by pure will alone. The same sheer will that was going to give her a life with Samhain the way that she saw fit. From what Elee believed, all she had to do was keep patience for the time that her love will come. Though how was only a test of how evident she was about herself and the priesthood?

The sound of the gongs banging caught her attention as she prepared for her scholars. Breakfast was now over and the lesson plans were soon to presume. The scholars chatted during their walk through the synagogue as they usually do. To them there wasn't a difference in activity and all was well within their studies. They didn't know that Elee would be giving the lesson because she never has.

Preparations would become evident to the scholars this

morning. They all poured in one by one and all of them were fully surprised about the arrangements. Never had the training hall been preset for any combative lesson, it was a beacon of a new becoming. Mostly the scholars were in awe about the sudden change and Elee knew so very well. She never left her state of meditation until the arrival of most of the scholars. Upon opening her eyes she, addressed the class for those who may not have known who she was. She rose from her seated position and then walked to the middle of scholars on the floor.

'I am pleased to meet everyone.' Elee insinuated.

Buckner wasn't too far from Sicily and Cash though he encouraged them to carry their hearing. He was familiar with priestess Elee and he had taken a wild liking to her. He had never seen a woman more beautiful or that smelled as sweet as Elee. He was more than open minded to her as he had felt that he was connected.

"Today is going to be a bit different," Elee had continued speaking. "We are preparing you for one thing that is constant in life, and that is change. I was asked to give this lesson plan due to the uncommon consistency of change. As you can see the arrangements of the weapons upon the floor are set for your personal uses. Preparations need to be you inner most consistency."

Buckner smiled as he hung to every word that left her mouth so fluently and sensually. He was enjoying the way that she was presenting her lecture. Even more he was simply enjoying being in her presence for the time being. He wondered if any of the others had felt the same way as him, yet the looks on their faces hadn't indicated the same. She began speaking again so he gave her his utmost attention.

"I have never taught any of you so I would like to know who is the strongest combative here?" Elee asked.

Again the scholars poured on more distraught stares then a suggested comment was made. Everybody knew that Buckner, Sicily, and Cash were the best at everything. Nobody wanted to stand against their own pride before Buckner had finally raised his hand. Sicily and Cash both followed in his lead, but only to claim the rightful stake.

"Is this it? Are you the top three scholars or the oldest ones among the group? Who says age isn't redefined at its best?" Elee inquired.

Elee pulled her hands to her face as if she was shocked. She took a good look at the other scholars who looked like they were preteens at the most. This was going to be a task a tad bit too advanced for them she thought to her. She took note of the scholars and figured that they could become a part of the lesson and begin schooling the others. Elee took hold of the three top scholars and had them stand next to her.

She began walking them all through proper combative techniques step by step. While doing so she used the scholars to demonstrate with each other before she allowed the others to take action. Buckner wasn't hesitant to become her right hand man in the task. He quickly offered his assistance in order to display his skill. Elee had to prepare him by adjusting his stance and body form. From there she asked him to rotate his sword to face his opposite hand and hold it straight out just above his head.

Elee assured him that the stance was to block a vertical strike as he noticed when she took a blow at him. The attack rattled his arm and thrust it back to him slightly. He hadn't imagined that she was as strong as she was and that she could stir him up the way she had. From that he drew to her even more.

"Don't let it become a surprise to you that an attacker could be stronger than you are. That's when you'll need to adjust to the pace of the fight and assess your own advances. Remember that the weapon is used to harm and kill over any other action at hand. Your life should become your will to endure." Elee said.

The scholars watched and nodded in agreement with her statement. They agreed that they would become responsible for their own lives. Elee began proceeding with the lecture that involved an example of how to interact within a fight. To her it was a visual of what a definite training session could build to.

Alright Buckner, this is it. Give your absolute all and attack me at will. Elee said.

Buckner's heart couldn't bare any more to be challenged, he didn't want to miss a beat with what was to be had by Elee's lesson. She had a wooden sword settled in her right hand that she extended to the body of Buckner. She was a prowess in tension and fear and the scholars could tell. "How amazing" Buckner had thought to himself as he showed a graceful smile. It was a first chance to prove to Elee how skillful and driven he was in comparison to the rest of the scholars. With both hands on his sword, Buckner tapped Elee's sword before twirling the weapon and going at her for a side slash.

His attack was well thought out and very wild yet still fierce somehow still giving Elee an advantage of a defensive maneuver. She wielded her sword to block the blow making a loud chopping noise as the wood connected together. The act that had left Buckner open and Elee took a side slash of her own that barely missed him. Buckner spanned wildly to counter the force as he delivered a second side slash that she dodged with great reflexes. Buckner fired off another slash that came horizontally at Elee's waist.

Elee was only trained by the best priest of times past and she was determined to display those lessons. She took the sword by two hands and wielded it upward then down in a vertical stroke. By her doing so, she blocked the slash but only before she had brushed him with the use of her shoulder and body. The force had pushed Buckner back a few steps and he noticed that she had him. She took another slash before his face that ran down his body.

"Alright, and thank you Buckner," Elee said.

"Wait is that it?" Buckner inquired. "I was just getting warmed up and I had you."

"Well we should draw into that at another time. Please return to your space. Now everyone we will practice striking on one another. As one strikes the other will work on blocking and vice versa." Elee continued to say.

Buckner sighed. He couldn't believe that he wasn't capable of topping over Elee in battle. It was less then what he hoped for in being a top scholar. How could he ever impress her if he couldn't even manage to keep up to her grade of skill? He walked to the sides of Cash and Sicily who both patted his back for the attempt. If he only trained more then he'll be one of the best, he thought.

Elee had directed everyone to pick a partner and Sicily suggested for Buckner's help. Everyone else was pairing up swiftly and they all had partners, everyone except for Cash that is. Being a top scholar had a downfall and it left him aside from everyone else. He told Elee as he looked confused about who he was to train with.

Elee smiled generously and comforted him. She proceeded in telling him that she knew she was going to have to be someone's partner and that she didn't mind helping him. Buckner wasn't too excited to hear that as he peaked over to listen to their conversation. Yet Cash grew excited and pleased over her words of concern. Not only had he found a partner, but he had the best partner around. Cash swore that he wasn't going to take it for granted and to excel to be better than Buckner.

Cash doesn't have any hard feelings for Buckner except for the fact that he couldn't get passed Sicily's feelings for him. Buckner was Sicily's joy as she was to Cash and it hurt Cash deep down. The moments to clear up any clouds of hope for his love for Sicily were drawing nearer each passing moment. Cash knew that his training session was to become a drawing of a real love and hate status for his feelings for Sicily over Buckner. If he doesn't do well how could she ever feel that she would depend on him for strength in a battle?

The first thing on Cash's mind was being labeled as a weaker scholar. It would have marked him for life to have to sit under one of the most subordinate labels ever. He was a champion and his face off with Elee was going to prove it to the whole priesthood. His thoughts conjured hard in his mind as he began focusing on approaches and movements to worry about. His patience had drawn a stare from Elee questionably because she focused on his deterrence.

Once the pairing had finished the other scholars began training at will though oddly Cash hadn't even picked up his weapon. It would've been intimate for him to fondle the wooden sword and began with a battle conversation to remote his less idled skills. But no, he hadn't said a word with his blank stare into the eyes of Elee. She imagined that his stare was creeping deep to her soul and into the abundance of her heart. The young adults face with eyes that were chill and as his wish would have it he began to slightly intimidate her. She began recalling her time as a scholar and the once high attitude of a drive to just fight and fight.

Elee began to wander about the scholar and what was driving his emotions. Again she looked inside of her own registered feelings at his age to only reveal that it was love that had moved her so aggressively. She acted in a meaningful attempt to spend as much time with Samhain as possible. Could she have been his means of reason to impress that he hoped to match wits with her? The ideas gave her a reason to blush, with thinking that her feelings would never unbind from her sights of Samhain.

"What stirred you so furiously that you wished to intimidate me with your cold and unjust eyes young scholar?" Elee had asked of him.

"My ability to adjust to battle is my only goal. This session will become one of my greatest tests!" Cash responded.

Without any doubt Elee hadn't wanted to sink any further to inquiries about the young scholars' goals. She continued in believing that she was his conquest, his only mean to becoming dominated. Elee was high about her beauty and she had realized the onset ideas that men wanted to conquer her heart. She figured that this scholar wasn't any more different from the rest of the men who desired her. She decided to play her card and remain calm against his approach.

Elee's regards for Cash were full yet she played to guard for her best interest within her heart. She didn't want to embarrass the scholar at the brink of his skill yet she forged her insight to be impenitent of his own. Dominance wasn't a greater perk to Elee anymore she appreciated her own respect at willful giving. Cash gave a daunting stare into Elle's eyes and her beauty had spoken to him gracefully as he hoped that she would appreciate his fighting skills.

"By all means, I am at your will to proceed at any given

time," Cash proclaimed.

Elee didn't respond with any sounding of words as she drew a smile that had warned with the cherry red stretching of her lips. Her movement began to flush Cash with great eagerness. A lean to her right was creating chills within his nerves. He settled on thinking to counter attack her assault without figuring how merciless she could actually be with her own skills. Cash wiped sweat from his palms against the pressure that he placed to his wooden sword.

His heart was racing in anticipation of what would become of this session. Nothing would hurt his pride any further if he couldn't amount to the hands of his teacher. It was time for him to show his might, skill and reserves. Elee kept hold of her sword with both hands placed onto the handle as it rested to her right side. Cash looked closely at how her waist was testily immobile, yet she began to lean forward with her right side.

"I got you," Cash roared indignantly. He gave an immediate curve to his sword to prepare for a vertical upward slash to Elee, that couldn't have been any more accurate. The attack led to Elee more graceful prancing around his attack. With another outward step to her right, she wielded her sword to take a side slash at Cash. Cash's move was immaculate but not enough to curve the edge of his sword to block her slash. Cash felt the blow of hard wood pressing against his side like a rock being thrown at him. He was fierce about not giving up. He prided himself in being fast enough to apply a thrust against her slash as he ran forward with the tip of his blade.

Only a few scholars had no reason to follow in watching the bout as Buckner, Sicily and the rest had all watched onward. Cash's friends have never seen him move with the type of will that he was displaying. To them he was the best of all of the scholars and this moment was priceless against any other.

"Wow, I didn't know he could move like that, very responsive." Buckner said.

"I know right," Sicily replied, "it's like he's really applying all his skills to prove himself."

"Sure, but that might not last for too long. I mean check out the priestess; she looks like she hasn't even broken a sweat yet." Buckner insisted.

"You know you're right. The both of them are moving at a high speed, but only Cash looks like he is actually tired." Sicily responded.

Priestess Elee adjusted her slash to counter Cash's thrust and aiding herself against puncture. Her back rolled against his giving her optimum advantage. Within her stride of movement her sword followed and began rising from between his legs. Elee's flow was so swift that Cash hadn' noticed the wielding blade until nearly at the last moment. After noticing the wooden shaft nearing him, Cash rested in his tumbling skill to backflip away from the priestess Elee.

Both Cash and Elee had once again separated from each

other's space. Even though the brush was a bit rough Cash knew that he had to move the course of the fight. He mimicked a stance given from lectures of Japanese sword fighting. His weapon was eye level to him with the blade balled forward. Elee wasn't bothered by his level of preparations; instead it had moved a shallow hole in her heart that she had doubted Cash.

"Time is still upon us if we are ever ready to continue." Elee claimed fearlessly.

Sweat beads rolled from Cash's forehead. His anticipation alone was over exerting energy that he needed to claim for himself. He knew well to believe that the possibility to overcome her was possible while she was in reach. Cash didn't allow his frustration to swallow his ability as he gave in well to his attack. From a few steps of reach he gave into a sideway slash that Elee had countered immediately. Cash sword flushed vertically, with his weight and using his force, he began pushing against the priestess.

Diverting the force had kept priestess Elee motioning backwards from Cash's level of strength. The younger man was much stronger than the skilled priestess, yet his brutal strength wasn't impressionable enough alone. Elee was known as being a sand priestess, her truest skill of being able to manipulate the sand and using it to her greatest advantage. The eyes of the priestess culminated a purple glow that raised questions in the minds of the scholars. What exactly was about to take place?

From under the feet of Cash the sand had begun to move. The driving force that Cash was giving had begun to weaken with each loss of his footing. The sand continued brewing as it lifted and circled the both of them. The beady rocks slammed continuously into Cash's face and body.

"That's not fair." Cash yelled uncontrollably. "I thought this was going to be a face off of whose skill was better."

"Doesn't this tactic drift to the elements of what my skills are at hand? My swordplay is only as great as my ability to warm a fight. If at all I thought you would have known that as a given acknowledgement of how to adjust to new situations. This is only another adjustment for you." Elee stated in high regard.

The sand began moving faster than what it had been going since its brewing. The mounds slammed into the body of Cash by chunks at a time. The flow was so rough that it began tearing bits of skin from all of his exposed face and hands.

"Buckner, tell him to stop!" Sicily demanded of him. She hated to see cash act like a stubborn brute. To her he does that to prove that he is able to go the distance with anybody, no matter how much it could hurt him.

"I don't believe I would even actually have to say in what way I can do anything about this one Sicily." Buckner commented.

The both of them knew Cash well enough to know that his determination is what keeps him winning. Just going further was his keenness at most, without his drive he would fall without fail. Cash was a fighter of fighters compared to all the other scholars. The sand twirled in devastating wrath that Cash didn't want to undergo any much further. His eyes illuminated and a red glow came from them and everything had stopped.

Everyone watching had just been struck with amazement of what was happening. They all had no choice but to realize that Cash had frozen Elee in time. The gorge of sand beads hovered in a shrouding cloud around them was like a curtain to Cash. He collected the sorted rocks and formed them into a solid ball that he aimed behind the head of Elee.

"What is he planning?" Sicily questioned to Buckner.

"Your guess is only as good as mine coming this time around," Buckner replied.

"What are you planning?" Buckner inquired to himself.

Only when he had believed that he had the fight working to his delight did Cash began to charm himself. He retook his position standing in front of the priestess before he released his freeze spell. Happiness is bliss and Cash was getting his full pictorial of how to enjoy it in full. The release of his spell had pulled the priestess toward Cash, whose surprise had caught up with him alone. The priestess took notice of her surroundings as she tilted to her left side.

The rate of motion was far too much for Cash to handle. The bundled sand ball came rolling fast toward the face of Cash. He yielded the blow to his face by separating the ball in half with a swipe of his blade. The action was almost consequential, yet apparent, that he had shielded his face from damage but to have drenched his hair and ears with mounds of sand. The arrangement of sand upon his body made a peculiar feature of an elf.

"Hmm, hmm," Priestess Elee chuckled at what she saw. "I never noticed how adorable you are with pointy ears."

A few of the scholars and even Sicily began laughing at the appearance of Cash. It wasn't an average view of him from any standard of opinion.

"I will admit that he is a bit more adorable this way." Sicily commented.

The laughter roared onward and nearly settled with Cash's anguish to fight. Now that he hadn't been able to land one connecting blows or even gained a settled upper hand. Cash was determined to show that he was a well prepared scholar of the tantric school.

"Enough with the compliments you will soon find this to be a difficult match," Cash proclaimed.

Something strange began to take place with Cash as his body had begun changing in shape. His face flattened then stretched outward, longing his mouth and arrangement of teeth. His arms, legs, hands, and feet all began to stretch to incredible proportions.

"You can shape shift?" Elee muttered softly.

"Did you know that he could do that?" Sicily had asked Buckner in disbelief.

"Yes actually, he's been practicing with me. Just last week he spent hours looking like me in the common areas." Buckner responded.

"Really, wow. How great is that? Way to go Cash!" Sicily proclaimed.

"This is child's play dealing with you young scholar." Priestess Elee pampered.

It took mere seconds for the youngster to fully complete his full transformation into a wolf hybrid. He look just like the enemy breeds except he had full brain functioning.

"How is this for a sparring partner?" Cash reclaimed.

With the extension of all of his viable muscles, Cash's body raised a few inches over his actual body height as he rose to six foot eight inches tall. His mass index had to have been well over two hundred and forty pounds of weight. With the gimmicks that priestess Elee was giving, he figured to carry on one of his own.

"Not bad beast. Everyone stand back much further!" Priestess Elee proclaimed to everyone.

The crowd was indeed amazed and evenly worried about the actions that could be taking place very shortly. The scholars murmured to one another beckoning the next one to move backwards as the crowd had expanded. There was enough space for the both of them to move freely enough in an engaging fight. The battle ground is set and everyone who was there had watched in anticipation.

Some of the younger scholars could be heard screaming that the wolf was going to eat them. The space was filled with a lot of fear at this moment; even Elee had lost a bit of confidence. The large beast with sharp fangs and claws could become way too much to handle for one night. Drool had run from the snarling mouth of the oversized beast. Amazed though irritated, priestess Elee when she started thinking about Maxin and what happened that awful night.

The best thing she can do, she thought, was use this moment to her advantage against the real challenge. Priestess Elee stood her ground in front of the six foot eight inch beast. She wanted him to start his assault of rage and death of dealing. She analyzed the being as being too large for her speed with a sword. Maybe she could dismantle him by limbs, she conjured.

It was as if it was the only choice to choose from auctioning. The arm of Cash had reached out in an attempt to grab hold of the priestess. Elee was well prepared for the thought of him grabbing her. With her wooden sword she swatted at the knuckles of the beast, then at his forearm. The attack wasn't forceful enough to stop his attack, yet strong enough to brush pressure into his arm.

The priestess had waved under the hand of Cash as she ran forward and smacked her sword against his bicep. The hit caused him to try to backhand the priestess as a countering hit. The large framed arm waved overhead of the priestess as she rolled beneath the waving arm. She struck Cash once again in the joints of his left leg as she rolled away from his attack. The blow had inadvertently harmed Cash as he stretched his upper torso to let out an alarming whelp. He screamed in anguish to overtake the priestess as she continued to swat at him.

"I will have you!" Cash claimed as he searched for the priestess' positioning.

The priestess wasn't even vaguely challenged by his comment at all. She managed to get behind Cash, before climbing his back, she brushed his legs with mounds of sand to bring him to a kneeling position. From then on she straddled the back of Cash as she began to choke him with her wooden sword. Cash tried to reach for her except that it laid no trending effect. The priestess was too out of place for him to reach, which she suspended her arms to dangle upon his throat.

Cash was in disarray as he focused in and out of consciences. Even in his overly large beast state, the flow of oxygen was very vital to his momentary use. He was helpless and out of resources to gather. The large framed beast fell harshly on his face before the priestess released her grip from his neck. Cash's form had come back to his natural shape during the heed of his exhaustion.

"Oh, is he alright?" Sicily asked in worriedly.

She ran to the side of Cash to aide his need for health. She rushed to check his vitals and to sustain him if she could. Her feelings for Cash had rushed heavy over her mind and heart. The priestess had noticed her concerns and tried to comfort Sicily with her composure yet Sicily didn't want any of the priestess support.

"Get away, you did this to him!" Sicily cried and pushed at the priestess. "You wanted to kill him because you were afraid of him, admit it."

Sicily cried further before the priestess had healed Cash's wounds. Both women came to a stare down of who's right was alarmed, though neither woman complained. Instead the priestess began speaking to the crowd of younger scholars.

"There will come a time that pure determination would be outmatched for the skilled execution. But it is during the battle that will give you that understanding. You will have to take control of what to feel and believe and that means keeping your cool and staying confident. No matter what your opponents' size is, it would take direction to deliver its defeat." The priestess said.

"Cash you ump." Sicily stated. "I thought you were going to die."

"No." Priestess Elee commented. "Not upon this day in time," She stated.

Cash draped his forehead back into the sand as he tried to meditate. He came to thinking about how wild and foolish he must have looked. Even knowing that all he had to give couldn't even present a dent toward the confidence of the priestess.

"I must have looked like a fool out there? Running wild against the skilled and highly trained priestess like that." Cash stated in defeat.

"Don't beat yourself up. I mean you are the best in our class other thank Buckner and I don't think anyone else would have done what you had just done back there." Sicily commented.

"Yeah, but I didn't give it much thought either, before I just did it." Cash replied.

"And that is why a seasoned veteran had to show you better. Determination wasn't enough for you Cash. You really had to focus on what would drive that determination to an uprooting of actual skill. If you could manage to balance the two then I would say that you're not that bad of a priest just yet." Priestess Elee implied.

Cash sat up with the helping hand of Sicily. She kept a firm hold of his hand as she knelt to his side. Her touch was comforting enough as he looked her over. She was a great supporter to him and it was times like this that made him remember that. Cash turned to face the priestess Elee before she had chosen to leave from his presence.

"Thank you, Priestess." Cash incited. "I believe I really needed that level of insight."

"Oh yeah, how?" Priestess Elee inquired.

"Your lectures and explanations is great stuff, and all the technical skills. But what I haven't learned through all of that was myself. The way you made me sweat had told me that I feared you, though my actions didn't want to believe that."' Cash implied.

"Wow. After our fight you came up with all of that." Elee replied.

"Actually, yeah." Cash sincerely stated.

"Well, you might actually have understood a new lesson called reasoning. If you don't reason with yourself then you can't get too much farther in any course of action. It takes that much of your full wisdom to draw to a better concept. Do you hear me Cash?" The priestess Elee asked.

"Oh yeah priestess. I'm clocking everything you are saying with great detail. It's going to take my pride some time to gather, but by then I would've thought twice as hard for a more driven plan of action." Cash stated.

"That's good thought for execution Cash, maybe I will get into teaching everyone my Air bending tech...." priestess Elee stumbled in mid conversation over the loud clutter that came from the main hall.

"Ugh, I heard roaring." The man said before stumbling to the floor. A pan had crashed to the walls as it trickled water through the sands on the floor.

"Maxin," priestess Elee cried out as she reached for his side. She lifted the priest to her shoulder to carry him to a near bench. The priest draped backwards onto the benches support, his body mimicked the actions of someone who didn't have full control of their muscular system. Maxin was in a great deal of pain and Elee couldn't figure out why he had to feel bountiful in his current state.

Priestess Elee tipped the head of the wounded priest Maxin at the moment he began to speak.

"Your voice had come over me. It echoed in my ears as I slept." Maxin said before swallowing the moisture that was within his mouth.

"You need rest, I can feel the thread of your heartbeat…" Elee commented shortly. The long and faint gasp that was forced by Maxin was hard to hear.

"Then that awful roar… That time forsaken cry. They despise the sound." Maxin stated.

Priestess Elee let out a shuttered gasp. Why was he talking as traverse as he was and who were they? "Alright Maxin, you're tired and you seem to be talking in circles." Elee said.

Priestess Elee lifted Maxin's head so that she could see into his eyes. The stare that he gave her was cold and dull. Priestess Elee took a dry cloth from her satchel to wipe his forehead.

"Why are you sweating so much?" Elee asked.

"The man said that it would be like this, he said I will die before anything else would take place." Maxin stated.

What he said had shocked the priestess, it caused her to give him an offensive stare of rigid countenance. He sure was acting weird again by saying that the man had told him that he would have to die when he's one of the strongest men within the school. Why he would be dyeing if so, wasn't an answerable question for the priestess. She knew better to consider his words as Maxin had fainted to using the last of his energy.

"Alright you all please continue with each other and you…" Elee demanded while pointing at Buckner. "Please help me carry him into his quarters, he's going to need his rest."

Buckner submitted to the priestess wishes and helped in carrying Maxin back to his living quarter. Out of the other scholars he was the only one strong and able to help support the weight of Maxin against the priestess. Buckner hurried to the left side of Maxin to turn him to his quarter as he took on most of the body weight. The priest lagged with most of his weight being lopped-sided by the priestess' inability to support him. Buckner rarely asked questions about the prism of the schools leaders, yet he became curious.

"Priestess Elee?" Buckner inquired.

"Yes," the priestess replied.

"So much has happened the past few days and I was wondering where Lord Samhain had gone to? Is everything alright with the school? Should I have to prepare the others for something to come?" Buckner asked.

Buckner's questioning had taken her by surprise so much that she didn't know how to respond. Everything wasn't fine, but she didn't want to startle the scholars by far. Her goal for defense wouldn't even be enough to settle in a statement, so she began to lie.

"You know what young scholar." She states.

"Buckner, my name is Buckner!" He replied.

"Yes Buckner, Lord Samhain is doing a perimeter run. We do them all the time and he wanted to check on things by himself," The priestess said.

"Okay but that doesn't explain what's wrong with priest Maxin and…" Buckner commented.

'And nothing. He's sick and we need to take care of him. Nothing bad is going to come out of this. It's only a time for healing, okay?" The priestess closed the conversation.

"Yes ma'am." Buckner replied.

"Just call me priestess, no ma'am. I'm no madam, my spirit's young and my soul isn't so closed-off, okay Buckner?" The priestess replied.

Buckner didn't reply to her comment as they approached Maxin's quarters. Instead he remained insightful by continuing in the priestess lead in carrying Maxin. A lit candle had warmed the entrance to his room where they had entered and laid the man to rest. Maxin's body temperature had fell heavily and his skin was very pale. It was something that Buckner wasn't used to seeing. Outside of class he had never seen anyone to ever succumb to something so detrimental.

"We must try to keep him warm." Priestess Elee stated while keeping calm. "Please grab his extra blankets in the corner behind you and we will bundle him up."

"Alright." Buckner said while reaching for the priest's blankets. "Should we tuck him in tightly to shut out the wind?"

"Yes, Buckner. We would want to do this as tight as we can get it yet the fresh air will also help. Afterwards you can return to the other scholars. I am going to brew some soup for him, I'm sure he can use the nourishment." Priestess Elee stated.

"Yes, priestess." Buckner replied. He finished tucking the priest in the blankets and adding comfort to his head by fluffing his pillow. "May I go now?"

"Thank you, and yes, you may go," she replied.

Buckner gave his regards to the senior priest before he left from Maxine's quarters. Something was alarming to him about priest, Maxin. Why wouldn't they just heal him like they would do on any regular case? Things didn't add up and he figured he should warn the other scholars for what devastation that could be just around the corner. He took a steady file approach back to reaching the other scholars because he wanted to try to think of optional plans.

~ ~ ~

"Why do you insist on telling me such lies about the Celtic Priesthood, these ideals of idolatry and passions of magic is not what the priesthood is about. We have a priesthood here in the Far City, yet this is not what they are about." Constable Greg insisted.

"But maybe you should just listen if you know so much!" Sasha implied.

Constable Greg excused himself one more time, at the moment that he attained a fellow Constable and asked him to report to the Celtic Priesthood of the Far City for questioning. He wanted to show Sasha that she was crazed, and diluted in self-imaginary ideology. Nothing could come to his City such as the possibility of magic and a cursive group of disturbing creatures.

"I'm back," Constable Greg said. "Now please continue."

"Where did I leave off ?" Sasha asked.

"This Buckner was speaking with the priestess and then…" Constable Greg said.

The time had shifted into another evening and Samhain had realized that he's been traveling for at least a day. The cave had led to a run-off that flowed under a waterfall that was kept by a large gorge. The run-off lead into a smaller town that held close to a few hundred people. The area was a large community that was well balanced of elders to youth. Few people who spotted him hadn't paid him any mind until he walked further into the small town.

He took notes about how well adaptive the people were in this area. They had multiple wells, a few barns and a yard for cattle to graze. It seemed that they had enough sustainable needs to comfort him through the night. Most towns kept a lodge for travelers to feast and sleep for the nights to come and he knew well to settle in. The main row in the heart of the community is where he had ended his moments of travel. The people there were the ones that took most action in community activities and was where he could learn more about the region.

Once he had entered the lodge he had received a great deal of the allotted attention from all onlookers. They watched the rivers water drip from his clothes to the floorboards. Many probably wondered what had brought him there as some others couldn't conceive the thought to question another person. His mind was focused on the lodge so he hadn't attempted to speak to anyone about anything.

A heavy set brunette woman was behind the bar counter to handle all financial transactions. She was tipping a drink for an older male customer when Samhain had reached the bar countertop. He hadn't bothered to take a seat at one of the bar stools. Instead he kept his focus on the brunette. The priest used his utmost respect while talking to the woman and he asked for a room for the night.

"This is Idel, the nearest city to the Far City." Constable Greg said.

"This is something that I too had to realize Constable Greg." Sasha said.

The brunette was excited to see that someone actually wanted to stay there. It was years that anyone had come to stay at the lodge and she was open for the rental value. Before extending her service to the man she became curious about his history. Why was the man wet and why had he ended up in the small town?

Samhain was the epitome of intellect and he closed the business owner out of his true reality.

He knew better than to tell her about the pack of wolves that just stayed miles away up the river. It would have devastated the small community as well as bringing greater attention to himself. Instead he lied and consented to the fact that he had slipped into the rivers stream and washed up on the embankment. As pleasant as he was the woman took full compassion for the disheartened man as she asked for the fifteen shillings rental charge. The lord priest was induced with money from the earnings that he had with the farm at the Sanctuary.

The brunette had left the bar and walked Samhain to the boarding room area upstairs. She encouraged him to buy a shirt and pair of pants as he would allow his clothes to dry in the cellar near the furnace. Samhain reluctantly agreed to pay the extra five shillings charge on top of the fifteen shillings. The exchange was worth it in his current state of needs. The closer that they had neared the room the more curious he had become about the roaming activities of the building.

Samhain had come to realize that he hadn't prayed in days and he needed his support from God. He knew to conclude himself exclusively so he didn't bother to ask the woman about livestock, at least not immediately. He inquired to her about the meals, he wanted a selective piece of raw lamb. The woman was confused about his taste in delicacy but with the two shilling charge it hadn't concerned her that much. They reached his room and the woman had gathered his clothing size before she assured him his meal to be sent to his room.

The dark priest was pleased and thankful for the assorted resources. The brunette left to get his clothes as Samhain retreated to his bedroom. He took his time undressing as he hung every garment in a small clothing closet. While he waited he began wondering about all the claims that had been undergone. The extraction of all human life was soon coming to light and something wasn't too becoming of it all.

He tried to think harder about it once a knock had raided his door. He fled from his concerns and rushed over toward the door. It was the keeper of the lodge. The well shape brunette was open-handed with clothes that she immediately handed to him. It was a fair exchange of smiles as both people had reached a moment of pleasantries.

It's been close to an hour past and the hailing moonlight shifted through the sky. The dark priest had gazed out of his window as he watched his lamb being slaughtered and prepared for his taking. Time was the most fluent thing running and the dark priest wanted to be able to get a hand on it. He tried to imagine the years to go by and what could be in store for his priesthood. It was awkward for him to think of it though in lost fractions.

His resurrecting soul could outweigh any average being yet he couldn't mind the full equation as to how. How could he manage to keep anything going without a firm indication? The trail had outlasted his time of thought when a knock came to his door. Assuredly he already knew it was the lodge keeper.

"Hello Sir. I brought the raw lamb as you had wish for. Is this the most that you had wanted Sir?" the lodge keeper asked.

Samhain was keen to her inquisition as he thanked the woman. He assured her it was fine but only before he asked how to reach the cellar to dry his clothes. The woman was easy going and non-expecting of negativity so she didn't suspect anything bad or wrong. The end of the hall had a door to the left that had a staircase that led to the cellar. The stairs curved on the first level beside a door that led to the back of the bar area.

It was perfect closure with great warmth of the furnace to perform a sacrifice. Being that the lamb was rightfully killed he encouraged himself to stir with the slab of meat. Samhain hadn't bothered drawing up a pentagram to perform his ritual rightfully. Instead he managed to keep with himself. Masterful in its use it made a beautiful second choice.

The lamb lay in the middle of the pentagram as Samhain kneeled and chanted softly. The chanting helped him gather strength as Satan, Gods counterpart has granted him more spiritual abundance. He continued until he had his fill of awakened power. The lamb then was to be braised in fire and brimstone as acknowledgement of the burning flesh in hell. This was to carry over satisfaction for when Satan detains the Earth with hell fire. Within the sacrifice it was to keep Satan satisfied of killing others.

At the finish of his praise the dark priest tossed the lamb

into the furnace as he began gathering his things. His leather coat was damp but nearly dry from the high temperatures inside of the cellar. There was a new face of life for him and he wanted to figure out how he would come to challenge it. The priest left the cellar and with an abundant idea of blending in. He spoke graciously to the bartender before he left the lodge.

This town was well suitable for some new actions. Samhain began to dream about how he could manifest his ministry and his slow triumph over devastation. The concept was grand yet the manifest was darkened by specific subject. How? He continued to ask himself during his stroll through town.

He began strolling past a farm that stretched for many yards. The large scaled area reminded himself of his land of cash crops that granted most of his wealth. He stopped to examine the structure of the area that held over a dozen different crops. The manifest of horticulture is an everlasting concierge that is a strong and solid foundation. He knows that the owner had to been a person of futuristic idealism.

Samhain continued in analyzing the yard and taking note of the crops being planted. Tomatoes, potatoes, onions, garlic, and fruits he began stating to himself. His voice was soft though loud enough to be heard by short ranges that a man had heard him. This man was quirky and shorter than Samhain but very well dressed in which he walked directly to Samhain.

"All of the most anticipated grids by the average person. The size of the yard is what really guarantees sales because it is in itself everyone's grade of want." The man said. "By the come of harvest the money is instant and as usual all the crops are sold. The best of it all is the …"

"Rice and wheat." Samhain concluded for the man.

"That is correct, mainly because of its storage ability." The man implied. "That's how I managed to make my living as a wealthy millionaire."

"You own this land." Samhain questioned the man.

"Indeed I do." The man replied.

"This place is only slightly larger than my fields and I don't understand how you can obtain millions." Samhain stated.

"That's because I sell certain fields for use and I rent my tools. The cotton, wheat and rice and fruits are my main crops that I sell regularly at all ten farm lands that I own." The man implied.

Samhain took notes of the man's just insight as he viewed the man's proportions. He noticed the slenderness of the six foot one-ish frame as he began to question his intellect. Oddly enough the man carried more intelligence than brute strength and that worried the priest. Has his stretch of reign succumbed to a single being that was more bountiful than his own god or even Satan? His matter for finance had made Samhain want to take over the man. He will have the need to build his future endeavor in this town and he knew that very well.

'I can use him is what Samhain had told himself. With a

stretch of his money I will be able to further the new location for the temples to come.'

"Excuse me sir, yet I have a question for you if you will have the time to talk with me?" Samhain proclaimed.

The man was open and very curious of what this strange man had to say. It was as if he procured to Samhain by him being new to the region. He deals with people regularly yet this one moment had taken his focus. What did the estranged man want to ask him?

'Sure I am a business man and I always feel very open to new discussions with people. Does it have anything to do with money? If it does deal with money, then I'd have to wonder if it was a business offer that you may have." The rich man said.

"About that…" Samhain replied. "When it comes to money the worst thing about it is that the Church always expects its fair share of service and recognition." Samhain implied.

"Well you don't say." The man replied.

Samhain knew by the way that he captivated the man that it was possible to consume his spirit. It was becoming late and times for the dark priest to pursue his keep.

"Yes. In my eyes the father has rested great strength, a power like no other." Samhain implied.

"What does that has to do about giving my money to the churches?" The man questioned Samhain.

The man's body was way too small to overcome the larger framed body of the dark priest Samhain. Oddly the man began feeling a bit discouraged as if he knew that Samhain was going to try to use him if he could. Why should he allow any negativity to consume him? Against the hands of Samhain he understood the discussion was over and that it was time for action. Silence had broken and Samhain hadn't spoken a word of what to expect.

Samhain's eyes had released a slight glow of light that had illuminated. The same glow came from his mouth upon him opening it. The man stood terrified by the spectacle and it had been too late.

"What are you doing?" The man asked before being placed into a slight trance. He stared into the eyes of Samhain further before the glow in his eyes had dissipated.

"Now do you believe me?' Samhain had implemented in telepathy.

"Your lips aren't moving!" The man exclaimed slightly louder over the silent night.

"This is what God has done for me my friend, he has gloried me with much power." Samhain implied.

The man carried much will about himself though this moment had taken him unwillingly. The man implemented no strength to carry faith that he began to bow in submission to the lord priest. He fell to his knees and reached for the feet of Samhain.

"Lord please, I beg of you. What is it that you will need of me in these troubled times? At this very moment I am here for your service." The man called forth.

At that moment nothing was clarified to the man the means of what would satisfy Samhain. Instead Samhain turned and began walking away from the praising man. His actions were cold and bottled up away from the man's balling.

"Prepare a Temple for the coming of your Lord. In it you will build one alter and a channel of tunnels that will extend throughout the city. By then you will have sealed the demands of your father." Samhain commanded of the man.

Tears seeped from the man's eyes as he watched the dark priest walking away from him. Samhain was yet still within the mind of the greatly wealthy man. The moonlight edged behind the man as its glow had faded upon a stream of gray clouds. Two men had watched from a yard away from where Samhain and their neighbor had interacted. From where they stood they haven't seen the illuminated rays of light that had emitted from Samhain.

The details of what happened were very odd and unusual to the pair. The most influential person in the city had been witnessed balling at the feet of a complete stranger. The men had concerns for the lonely man whom they have known for years. The two had decided to approach him and ask the wealthy man if he was alright.

"I must go to complete the lords wish and finish my duties." The wealthy man said while rising to his feet.

The two men had heard him say as they approached him. His comment was odd at the account that they knew the wealthy man was an atheist and that he hadn't had a belief for religion. But why? How could he have developed such an engulfed attitude within a short moment's time?

The wealthy man began walking away but not before the two men asked if he was fine. He commended back to the men that he has seen the light of God and that it was time for him to aid the great lord's duties. The range of interest was minced within the two men who didn't come to understanding the drastic change. Why have the richest man in town had gone aback and settled in a new belief. To the men they figured that the possibilities were limitless and that they should try to find out more about the man whom they just saw.

"Why does it sound like this set of run in may actually mean something for this near future that you are drawing to." Constable Greg said.

~ ~ ~ ~

Howls coursed over the darkened sky and it almost seemed as if there was a certain chill that made a person cringe at the stealthy breeze of wind. What was going to be a wonderful night had been infected with a gruesome oncoming. The sanctuary was filled with many tired young children that couldn't wait to lay to rest within the comforts of their own beds. The laughter had taken strolls throughout the halls of the sanctuary as if it echoed onward.

Priestess Elee was spending time bathing in lavender oil and cherry blossom flowers. A scent that was lush and very silky across her skin that had favored her so well. Out of the hours of the day it was the most relaxing and nurturing when she enjoyed her bath time. A unescapable calm would always come over her when she would dream of the times that Samhain would come to her and yield her peace that she figured that she would always enjoy. Bathing was an oddity to her that takes her focus from the strains of reality, a reality that is out of her control and causes the majority of her concerns.

A follow up of how she couldn't conclude to a bigger picture of godliness. Her night was short of what she believed when the unthinkable had taken her by surprise. The mysterious six foot six shadow that beveled in the candle light had walked into her presence.

"This day was long and I have many great things to speak of yet I haven't indulged into the finer of those things. Things that many people may consider the best of indulgences.' The man said.

The priestess was already overtaken with much delight before she decided to beg for the companionship.

"Your comfort is mine as mine is to yours and this is a time that we should share together." The priestess said.

The level of conversation like the one that they had would discourage an average listener. Priestess Elee was above average and above all distinguished differences. The stranger was giving her the last of his heavy breath and full insight. To her his words were like a thorn that had uncovered the ark of her.

Priestess Elee was in a battle with death and the vanity that she ordained so well. Her last wish for death will be beyond the time that she controls. The scented oils of lavender stretched further beyond the halls of the sanctuary. It harnessed an element of a peaceful grace that deemed innocent. The time the two paired had matured and the six foot man had left the priestess alone.

Resting and now fully awake Maxin had incurred the lavender scent. The sweet fragrance had reminded him of Priestess Elee and his remembrance how stunning she could be in her garb that wrapped neatly around her breast. He encouraged to himself the ruminant of her heart and how well it pumped of flushed pure red and translucent blood. The priestess was sitting up waist high in her bath while brushing her hair. Her neck tickled of a fine touch that raised chill bumps down the spine. The feeling was cold and eerie that it caused the Priestess to jump in an upstart of hysteria.

To her surprise her hair had caused the chill due to the soaked touch of the multiple strands. The priestess wasn't feeling comfortable by the spiritual hold within the atmosphere. A soulful resign had changed and it raised her attention of awareness. What has changed had stumped her, yet she knew to check on the others in the sanctuary. A few days in leadership and the absolute feelings of comfort had seemed to surpass her thoughts.

Wholeheartedly the priestess had accepted her responsibility and didn't want to under step in her walk of the position. She quickly rose to get herself dry and clothed. A few minutes time had passed when she finally finished wrapping her hair into a bun as she would do regularly. Her left hand held onto a candle that burned bright enough to light a few feet ahead of her. Her right hand was firmly gripping a wooden sword that she figured that she would paddle at the rears of her scholars who haven't attempted to rest yet.

She made no mind to think if Maxin was awake or not. His body had drained him so terribly that his resting was a given. A cold chilled breeze rushed past the priestess as it brushed her face. The blow nearly forced the candle out, causing it to flicker wildly as the flame fought to stay lit. The priestess then shielded the light with her right hand while holding tightly against her sword.

The breeze was unnatural, being that the sanctuary was sealed in. The priestess had shrugged her shoulders in the midst of her concerns. The quarter of the scholars wasn't too far but only steps away from where she stood. The priestess had expected a great deal of commotion coming from the scholar's room. She made a bid to herself that they felt as if they had more authority to do as they may please.

She figured her thoughts were behind and lost wildly once she had noticed that all of the scholars were fast asleep. The onset was hard to believe at the time since she knew for sure that they could have been disobedient. Without any doubt the priestess was excited for the scholars as she hoped for all of them that they would be great students under her tutorship. They were hers to nurture and nothing would keep her from doing just that. The priestess began closing the door but soon after she had run into a surprise.

Maxin leaned heavily against the wall barely holding his self-up. He had startled the priestess to almost believing that he could have been a foe in an attempt to harm her and the scholars. Her duty to her brother was needed as she rushed to aide him. She grabbed hold of his back and wrapped his arm around her neck.

'Brother, you shouldn't be walking in your ailing condition, why have you moved?' the priestess asked.

"By this time I wouldn't have believed." Maxin stated softly.

The priestess lifted the higher ranked priest and continued on carrying him to his quarters. Solely she tried to follow and understand his words except that they weren't complete or making any sense. His statements were open and not conclusive, this wasn't the first time he had spoken this way.

"What is it that you are trying to believe brother, I truly don't understand?" The priestess stated.

"The power that I have succumbed to, "he mumbled," the glory that has been given to me by the night. The glory of a greater atonement is upon me." Maxin stated.

The priestess was confused by Maxin again, what was going on with him she wondered? He's terribly ill and he's talking about being more powerful. The larger frame of Maxin was creating a great strain on the priestess and it caused her blood pressure to rise as her heart rate impeded.

"The sound is calling, and they would like me to show you what I mean." Maxin stated.

His words rang in her ears like a sharpened piece of steel that shredded upon each grating word. She doubted his sanity and paid his unintelligible ravings no mind. Unluckily Maxin was zealous in action in gripping the priestess with his powerful strength. His superior force pushed on the priestess even while he was ill was still enough to keep her from moving forward. His mouth gaped widely with two oversized fangs that draped from his upper row of teeth.

The priestess screamed loudly that roared an echo within the sanctuary. Only a few of the scholars had heard the scream while the others slept deeply. Maxin had forced the priestess to a wall as he drained her of her blood. It was as if he was stealing her energy as she cringed and screamed more. The awakened scholars rushed to the others as one had brushed Cash.

"Cash, something is wrong with the priestess, please come and help her quickly." The younger scholar demanded.

The room then had been awakened as Cash screamed in alarm. He led everyone to the hall where Buckner and Sicily had soon followed. To their eyes the scene was sternly shocking to see as the priestess was being drained of her essence. A true moment of clarity for Cash stood before him as one of the top scholars. He ran to the priestess in hopes of helping her, but was shortened by a backhand to the face. The blow forced the scholar backwards into a crowd of younger scholars as they all fell backward in a rally. The relaxing grip from her shoulder had allowed the priestess time to gather her wooden sword. With enough strength to grip onto the training stick she then jabbed the edge into the sternum of the brutal priest. The blow caused the priest major pain as he yelled in agony. He released his grip from her as she fell to the ground.

Both the priest and the priestess whimpered from pain that stabbed at the source of their wounds. Ineffective in action they both fell in a state of silence. The priest reached for the blade that hung from his chest in a means to remove it. Cash felt unsettled by his attacker that he sprinted to only crash into the handle of the blade, therefore driving it further into priest Maxin's chest. The blade moved again thus pushing itself into the heart of Maxin.

Maxin scowled from the pain and was forced into a stumble. The powerful priest fell to his back as blood flowed from his body. His body moved in a short hemorrhage before calmly taking rest to death. Cash had never killed anyone nor seen a person that was dead. The view was extremely shocking that he watched the priest for moments before remembering the priestess.

The priestess hadn't moved for a while and her pain was excruciating. The group of scholars had all cast their eyes upon her as some cried and whimpered.

"Please Cash, heal her," Sicily cried out.

Cash was clammy and nervous about helping the priestess

in stopping Maxin. He wasn't too sure if healing her was something that he could do at the level of pain that she was in.

"Please Cash, Please." Sicily continued.

"Okay," Cash responded, "I'll try."

Cash had built up his aura as he began channeling his energy. The bright red rays channeled between the scholar and the priestess as energy began to engulf her body. Perspiration had settled on the brow of Cash as he grew even clammier. It was more of what he had thought even though he continued onward.

"Sicily help me, it's too much!" Cash reached out.

Sicily had grabbed hold of Cash shoulder; her aura was low but supportive. Immediately Buckner steps in to channel his aura as well. The other scholars could see that as they all began taking hands with each other. Together they all forged to make the aura channel with numbers in strength that changed the color of aura to green. Gravity itself couldn't pull her any closer to life. The priestess gasped for breathe of air at her regaining of life.

"I can't believe it!" The priestess stated.

Her body then repressed in shock, sending her into a moment of sleep. The scholars had stopped channeling their aura at the moment of her faint yet their hearts were sorrowed once again.

"Will she be alright?" Sicily asked frantically.

The scholars were speechless and unable to answer her question due to the unknown extent of her injuries and healing. What was going to happen next? Who will lead the group? Where is Lord Samhain and when will it be that he returns? The inclusion had awakened the spirits of the older scholars.

"So the man bit this woman yadda, yadda, yadda with this grave amount of detail. It does not concern me. I only wish to know what has happened earlier this night and that is it." Constable Greg asks.

"If you would ask again this story is what I will tell to you in the same manner." Sasha said.

~~~

Oddly Samhain continued in walking through the open terrains of the small town. Candle light loomed in the distance of every reaching corner that he stood facing. His objective was clearer than the direction that was leading his up to his satisfaction. At times he felt as if another force was driving a path of challenge that steered him to his victory. His focus was surely set to continue onward when he came to an end of the city's border.

In a distance there was a glowing that he knew too well. It was the bright sectors of fire lights that would've been used in towns or homes. The curiosity of the dark priest hadn't faded too much further from finding newer discoveries. If there was anything in that general direction it would surely mean something. A leap of faith challenged the dark priest in continuing across the bridge.
~~~

In the midst of his anticipation, the dark priest hadn't known that he was being followed. The two men that befriended the rich man had kept a close watch on Samhain. In a graceful eye they followed him into the sectioning town. With only a keen sense of sound the two men had followed the weaving breathe and the pounding of Samhain's shoes. The three men had pressed into the town where nobody was awake.

Samhain continued in his scouting of the region to only come across a few dozen homes and a small cattle farm. It became unlikely that anyone was going to greet the dark priest. He soon then began to encouragingly challenge himself. The priest snuck into the farm and stole one of the baby sheep that was deep in rest. The beast neighed in fear and it startled Samhain so much that he snapped its neck. Away into the woods a distance from the town, Samhain cleared space to draw to God once again.

The men that followed were not afraid of the dark lords' actions but only curious. They watched him create his pentagram with the sheep's blood. After doing so he created a sculpture with mud and the blood of the sheep. From his pocket he pulled out his orb to engulf his sculpture. From his call to God the mud sculpture began to take form into something alive and real.

The priest continued conjuring and the figure began to appear. It grew of larger proportions of human and beast like features together. The two men stood amazed to see a power as they had. Afraid, both men were curious as to what was in store.

"Must you tell me more about this magic?" Constable Greg

interrupted.

<div align="center">~~~~</div>

Buckner had led the scholars in the late night discussions for what to think. Together they had already moved the priestess to her quarters to rest. The remains of Maxin laid wrapped, mummified in old garbs laid restively behind the sanctuary in the yard. Discussions began to reign openly and not discreetly among the scholars. Topics that questioned who will lead and what are they going to do next?

"It's getting late everyone and I already came to the conclusion that we should have the best scholar to lead in our formalities. One thing is for certain we all see that Cash is the one to lead us. I don't want to have to consider age because…" Buckner stated before being cut off.

"Why shouldn't we consider age for canididacy. I think age would've been the best of all reasons." The scholar stated.

"Alright, but I would like to admit that you haven't come to being a priest either." Buckner replied.

"Boo hoo, I'm still the largest, smartest and most seasoned around here and it's about time I got some respect for it too." The scholar demanded.

"Look I'm going to do this, we're going to have a vote of who should lead us until the priestess or lord Samhain returns. All hands for the older guy.' Buckner asked.

A lot of hands had drawn that looked closely to more than half the group of scholars. Buckner and Cash looked around with amazement to see the number of scholars whom voted against him. The looks of the crowd was a no brainer yet the question still had to be asked.

"Alright with a showing of hands can anyone tell me who wishes for Cash to lead us?" Buckner stated.

A smaller array of six hands had gone up, and quickly showed the diversity. To whom of all was right, seniority had taken the hand to be. Cash didn't shy away from the reasoning, he only converged it with dignity and respect for the senior. His thoughts were simple and just to allow the upper hand to take refuge.

"Ha, I told you so." The senior praised.

"You know I haven't any real doubt Buckner. He has a few years of gratitude and what do I have? Nothing but sure will." Cash explained.

"Sure you can say that buddy, but you actually excel further and I believe that the duty should have been yours." Buckner proclaimed.

"Well after all this is said, somebody is going to have to take a night watch and who else better but the runner up and his guards." The senior said.

"You mean us?" Buckner questioned.

"Definitely!! You two work well together and I'm sure you

can manage to keep each other company." The senior replied.

Buckner and Cash both gave each other a glance before letting out a sigh. It was a given that the two were tired and ready for rest yet they've been lead to a responsibility.

"Well I guess I'll stay up with the both of you. I mean two can easily fail though three can conquer in portions. So how about it?" Sicily asked.

"Yeah." Cash and Buckner both responded.

"Alright I'll grab blankets and pillows then I'll meet everyone in the hall." Sicily stated.

"That's fine, we are…" Cash said staring at Buckner.

"..going to check on the priestess." Buckner insisted.

"Good idea. I'll be there in a minute." Sicily stated.

The two male scholars left their room in leading the process of guarding the compound. The walk to the priestess quarter was sustainable with no regard to the incident from before. They may though fear an encounter more than anything else though they kept faith in conclusion between each other.

"So don't spend too much time sleeping like babies while we babysit for the night." Sicily commented to the scholars.

One of the younger scholars made a comment to her from her bed. The young girl was around nine or ten years of age and was very furious.

"I'm no baby." The girl shot back.

Sicily was shocked at the girls' indisputable response and could tell how challenging it had been for the younger scholar. Being that the girl had grown it still didn't outweigh the fact that she didn't have to take Sicily seriously. The sarcasm of Sicily had divided the younger girl to a less connective category of conversation. Though Sicily took that as a chance to outline how important it is for her to regroup at this point in time.

"Sorry sweetie, I meant that as an understatement." Sicily said.

"Oh, well that was above me," the young scholar replied.

Sicily nearly cracked a smile and reverted from doing so. She took into mind that the little girl really didn't know what Sicily was speaking in full meaning about. She didn't want to allow the young girl to become a distraction to her duties. Sicily excused herself from everyone else after asking if they wanted the window open for a breathe of fresh air. The scholars all agreed in the comfort of the fresh breeze to cleanse the stained air within the room.

Sicily quickly left while leaving the window in a hands width open. The cold breeze easily gushed in and left everyone reaching for their blankets. As cozy as it could have felt Sicily wished she had the same option to go by. Her adherence to the mess hall had opened her thoughts to a drawn out night. Nothing was conjuring in her head when she approached the priestess quarters.

Buckner and Cash was seen easily tending to the priestess side. It became an eyeful of encouragement to why she pleads to do more and more for the both of them. The three were a team never any less than any of the other groups that could say how well they knew their players. Her approach was meek, as she brought the sleeping gear for everyone.

"How is she coming along?" Sicily asked while dropping everything.

Buckner gave Sicily a worried look with a form expression of concern Cash was holding his hand against the priestess forehead to check her temperature. He'd expected her body to be warm from her clothing, though he was wrong. She was cold like ice as if her humanity was fading away.

"She's practically frozen," Cash stated." We would need to keep her warm."

"I can get Maxin's old blankets." Sicily indicated.

"That would be fine." Cash replied.

"Something isn't right guys. This is exactly how Maxin was before he started acting all weird and stuff. I tried to think long and hard about it but it all wouldn't add up right. They didn't heal Maxin because he couldn't be healed." Buckner stated.

"What are you saying Buckner? That he needed to be cured. Is this the reason why Samhain left us all here with them, to find a cure?" Sicily questioned Buckner.

"I don't know exactly, but what has happened to Maxin is going to happen to the priestess next!" Buckner implied.

The open air gave to a faint cry for the whooshing wind that brushed Cash's face. In the mix of his rhetorical thinking he began wondering about the options for the sanctuary. Without a great minded leader to open up the doors to a sovereign lesson plan, they were going to be behind in future events. The group knew well that things could easily become derailed if they were the leading activists. Everything that they knew came from the lessons from the elder priest and now they had nothing.

"How about we don't try to worry about that right now and we stick to protecting this sanctuary. By the time things become too rough, we would've managed maintaining a provisional lifestyle for everyone here." Cash said.

Nobody commented because of the level of grievance that had combined over the last few conversations. No one was for sure about what to expect except that all they had at this point was each other. They all tried to better the night by discussing more about how to hold up in battle signature. Sicily was most curious on how to handle the blade of a sword though, it never came into play. Nobody was that eager to devise the action and yet they began to settle on things that were more mental.

If at best Cash wanted to teach Sicily and Buckner their transformation technique. They hadn't known it and Cash was the only one who really knew the extent of it. He brought up the story of how he got the technique from one of Samhain's manuals. The mental base acolyte that manipulates the energy within the body's cells, as Cash had explained it in full cause the transformation. The process starts with the thought and it inverts to the way you convert your energy.

"Ha, ha," Sicily laughed.

She claimed that it was all too unreal to believe and she wouldn't if she hadn't seen it done before her own eyes. Cash agreed that the influence was a bit damp, yet still rare to adhere to. It will allow you sustain any mammal form that derives from the use of blood cells.

"So you mean I can't turn to a three headed creature like the Cerberus or Medusa?" Sicily asked.

"Any bodied form." Cash had responded. "It's not just the form though the strength that it will take to manipulate the form to be honest the easiest form of all would be the human form."

"You mean… a person. Why?" Sicily asked.

"It's easy to say because you don't have to adjust to gradual strengths or other residuals. Mostly said if you ever try to manipulate an animal's form you would have to adjust to the bodily functions. It may sound easy now but the all honesty about it is the truth. In the end it takes a bit more energy and a wad of control." Cash said.

They took in the subjective lecture notes and thought more to harnessing the values. You could see within the faces of Sicily and Buckner that they were trying. They began showing differences in features from color, to teeth size and having spotty hairs. The transformation didn't stop with just that, yet the form of their hands had commenced as well. The will was there though it wasn't at all strong enough for Sicily, as she tried to shift into a wolf.

For Cash to explain it Sicily had lacked control over all of her body parts. The action was a full body coercive act and they only managed to pull from their certain cells. She shifted periodically and displayed the least of her powers. She began to notice the difficulty in the process it only encouraged her to understand the will power of Cash. His use of skill with his ration of reserve was his base for action.

"I tried to tell you. It's not the easiest act to pull over yet it is very extensive to follow through." Cash replied.

"Well for that matter, I would have to continue trying." Buckner stated," we both would have to." He said while aiming a look at Sicily.

Sicily smiled with a blind reserve as if the trial would've been tremendous. Her heart nearly floated as she thought further more about it. She then began admiring Cash a bit more. He was her release of action and beginning of a new on look. If she told him so then how would he respond to her?

She kept her affections to herself and didn't take any interest to giving in to them. In her mind she knew well that it would be time that will pull him to her. She continued watching Buckner and Cash discuss what was going on. She leaned in further to

Buckner's thoughts that handed them heavy ideas. It seemed that something was lurking in the mist and they knew nothing about it.

~ ~ ~

"What is it?" Jasper yelled out.

The loud knocks at the door had upset the man whom to all was the wealthiest by all accounts. The open spaced home that was filled with lavished furniture had echoed at the banging noises. The sounds seared like a roaring wave that crashed at the drums of his ears. Jasper's hearing was well equipped and could span a distance that no other could imagine. In a meaning to say he was much more different then the wolves themselves.

"Master, I have horrible news." The man said after opening the door and taking a look at the well gainful man.

Jasper's eyes had flared in alarm as they widened with depth. He disliked words like horrible, bad or worse because they carried a negative vibe, usually a distilled source that implemented a wrong doing. Jasper was mindful and couldn't understand any reason for a failed plot, especially his own.

"By account after account of restless mornings that have come and gone to leave me open to my wealth you and I both know that you plan to tell me something. Only by my saying something I underlined the conclusion that it's not anything that I would want to hear." Jasper had stated.

At the most he gave the predecessor a wild furrowed look

into his eyes, his pupils expanding wider with a fierce red color that showed his level of irritation and anger. His eyes were oversized and with no concern for 'bad' news. The male servant tried not to stare too long into his eyes. He tried turning away to formulate how he would inform his master of the leading news.

"Uhm, yes." The servant stated while explaining in high detail about how he first entered the sanctuary. His detail was very descriptive about how he took notes of the children as they began to sleep. They laid in numbers in wait of his approach to attack a few of them. From underneath the door a light had loomed in a fade as someone had approached. He described the priestess and how she had entered the room to a gaze at them all.

The conversation continued with the servant crawl clinging onto the ceiling and above her as he flew into Maxins' room. He gave the detail of how he whispered to him from above that "they must taste death". From then Maxin awakened in an unstable crawl that led to his approach to the priestess. He gave notes as to how she had carried the priest in his aide and his attempt to overcome her. Jasper wasn't liking the direction in which the conversation was turning.

"By now I would bet you would want to tell me that in some way that Maxin was killed. " Jasper states in a rising tone. He grew more upset with how he began to dislike the conversation. In anger he rose his hand before the servant in an attempt to strike him.

"But sir, before she killed the priest he was able to implement his mark to her." The servant said.

The story had tied in more worth and truth by the servant underling the turning point. It was then that Jasper had begun believing that his mission wasn't lost. With the priestess undergoing the turning process the Sanctuary was still open for his taking. With his lasting words the servant had retreated from Jasper's clutches unharmed.

"I see, yes." Jasper stated. All is not lost and I may still be able to ensure the destruction of the priesthood. After them the wolves would be the ones to follow in possession."

Jasper gave an uneasy look at his servant that revealed some sympathy. His new plans were streaming through his mind like running water. It was time to keep things on schedule and he couldn't wait to do it.

<center>~~~</center>

The night was shifting to colder and the dark priest was being catered to by his new servant Natu. The non-human creature favored the size of a bear and non-optional tended in Jasper's list of commands. Smoke began clearing from the scoured trees within the woods by the time that the two had moved from the area. It would have been treacherous in any moment for the two men to approach the priest. Instead they followed them again in the distant shadows that lingered around. "Natu," Samhain had said.

Natu grumbled in anticipation of what there was to know. His vow to Samhain was indefinite at the lasting of his own creation.

"This area; my dear servant of a creation. This is the resting of your new life of being. A region that you can call your own and where you will barter our greater finance. How does that sound to you Natu?" Samhain called out.

Natu gave into the suggestion and began examining the surrounding area. Just the thoughts alone had begun to nestle nicely with Natu. He smiled cheerily to the hopes of his reign. The stare at his massive size had told him the future of his worth to being pure truth.

"I will do so in a likely manner." Natu had agreed.

The pair continued forth in the walk to the bridge that separated the town from the city. Samhain led the way to the bridge that connected the two areas together. Midway across the bridge Samhain stopped to give way to Natu. The both of them had examined one another, noticing the significant differences.

"This here bridge Natu," Samhain stated. "This will be where you alone will extract your financial gain. If you are wondering how then I must tell you. You will embrace a bargo and you will take money from everyone that comes across it. Now how does that sound to you?"

Natu took a moment to look over the surrounding areas once again. He allowed the area to amaze him by the significance of its size. Animals squeaked and chirped as the nature became a sure sight to take recognition against. Trees had swallowed the distant hillsides and gorges. A stream trickled easily beneath the bridge that flowed with the oceans salt water.

"Natu will enjoy this new embrace of life." Natu stated.

Samhain threw Natu a heavy smile for encouragement in order to encourage him. By all means he was and he began realizing Samhain was about to take flight. In the midst of business to do Samhain was on his way to the large city. The two men and Natu had all watched the priest walk to the entrance to the city. He faded into the swallow of darkness that led away from the bridge.

Natu was firm still standing midway of the bridge staring in a dead gaze at Samhain. The enlightenment to control toll over the bridge became his new founded life goal. Life was simple and less subjective for Natu by his means of desires. He was less comforted by companionship nor did he have a want for money in his life. Nothing but a meal would open to his sub conscience need of life itself.

The two men from the city were a bit stuck in claiming what actions to take against the monstrous creature. They figured it would've been best not to impose any action at all. Alone they knew that the being would take to a place of peace on its own. The men decided to trail to the opposite side of the town where Toe River closed in and where they could find a scale-able ledge. The two decided not to tempt the worth of their lives with a loss in a determined fight.

Samhain was long past the sights of Natu and the two men that had trailed him. His freedom was seeking closure for his worth in the small city. Evenly enough he wasn't prepared for what was going to happen in the time to come. The lasting manifestation within his mind was to re-collect the orbs and use the power to construct his ultimate legion. Solely the purpose was for the case that he ever needed to use the dynamic force.

"A legion, a legion of what? If I may consider asking in question?" Constable Greg stated.

He was emptied by less adequate thoughts of either terrorizing or destroying anything within the region. A new flash of insight had domed the mind of Samhain. What if he could force an outcome to deliver his liege of companions? How could that satisfy his taste for full devotion from those that haven't yet spoke his name? Samhain's goal for dominance wasn't his decision to fight off his high number of sorted enemies.

During his walk he began giving thoughts to who or what demonic being had taken a pledge against his sanctuary. The truth would lead to a foreclosure of how he wished to anguish his plan to reform his sanctuary. But why or who had to retain any reason for doing so? It was ideal in understanding the truth that he only counseled with wolves on various occasions. From then on he hadn't yet to believe of any other force around to deliver any devastating blows to his faction.

The walk back to his room had become a bit uneasy for him. Samhain began feeling paranoid about the level of closure that surrounded him. The sunken night had taken shade across the land and every inch of space that was ahead of him. Without a sterile sight to view any type of interaction, the dark priest was still keen to his hearing. The stilled sounds of birds chirps was easily trampled over the rustling of leaves in the wind.

Samhain had suspected a difference but he couldn't quite land any idea to the source. It felt as if he could sense a new energy that wasn't normal. The priest had stopped to take a view of sight to the location that held the bottled energy. To his appeal he couldn't manage locating a single isolated being to the nature of the energy. Time began closing and he knew that he would have to move onward if he wanted to reach the bar in time for late night drinking.

His pace could be seen afar from the eerie source that lurked in the dimness of nature. The eyes followed him to his steps beyond the edges of a fence that bordered off to his left side. A gloom in the distance showed his way from a torch that flared in the middle of the field.

~ ~ ~

Howls had steered in an echo of the cave that the wolves had laid to rest. They rallied to stir morale in one another as they drew to each other as strength. The roars roamed from each other to the walls and then out to the distant woods. Together they formed the new revolution that had handed them a new foundation. A foundation of wolves that settles as a beacon to underline the regions past correlation of now and then sites to where the wolves had lived. All together the pack had formed into a circle within the dimly lit cave. A carousel of glowing eyes had filled the space as they all gazed on toward Lucky. Lucky who posted on top of a shifted rack that laid smack in the middle of the pack, was the leader. The she-wolf was prowess in comparison to the others with her intellect alone. The furred, large toothed, bug eyed beast began manipulating her form as her teeth retracted.

Her hairline followed in receding finely to her skin as her eyes retracted to regular size. The carnivorous beast is once again human as her body blossomed in full naked stature. The woman wrapped herself in a cotton woven cloak that covered her evenly. She was in the eyes of all the wolves that stood present.

"Hail lord Lucky, chief of the pack," they grumbled in a monotonous growl.

Lucky heaved herself at the onset of the gathering, engulfing the stigmatic energy. Cheerily, she smiled devilishly with vile looks to her pack.

"Shhh," Lucky finally answers to the crowd. The pack had followed in complete silence as mouths closed and ears flailed to the comparison. Lucky was in control of everyone around that was seen.

"The day of homage is pressing. The time to nurture one another is upon us. Alone we are weak, alone we are empty, lost, scared, and fearful. Though together we are one unit." Lucky said causing uproar.

"Together we are the solidarity beings of this land and all regions around. Without one there isn't the other or anyone else in the pack. We've lasted through the years against the priesthood and now what? We pressed on to rebuilding what was once lost among our prestigious group and recreated a new foundation!" Lucky shouted.

Howls whistled swiftly among the walls of the cave as other wolves panted in a happy slur to rally their spirits.

"Tonight is a new bringing of greater things that can only be defined by God alone," Lucky stated.

In front of the rock that she stood was the orb that Samhain had left behind. It was wrapped up in a cloth to shield it from everyone's sight. Lucky had lifted it up to the air in a wielding way. It amazed the pack as they scurried in circles at the sight of it. The most of them had seen the worth of orbs as to the others they were tempted to find out.

"A new dawn is coming upon us. By the time that we track Samhain wc would have him give us the way to unify the powers of this mystical orb. Together we will find a way for us to be stronger even at our weakest time of the day. We will forge to find a way to keep the inner beast at our will regularly and within the trails of day break." Lucky stated.

Roars and howls panted evenly at the statements given by Lucky. She had encouraged the will of perseverance among her ranks. She had lifted their spirits as she had done so continuously throughout time. To them the focus was pleasurable and would demand emanate dominance against all sides of evolution. At this point there wasn't anything behind them yet only the things that were before them.

"Our path in life is now been found, and at sun fall tomorrow we will have our eyes set for the new beginning of life. A new beginning of a generation of feral beast to freely roam the world, a world filled with beast." Lucky cried.

They all swarmed ferociously as they bounced off one another in a frenzy. Lucky spoke warm words that tapped the hearts and spirits of the pack, enlightenment that had settled deeply within the core system, the powers to be.

~~~

The morning sun had shown through the windows with the vibrant rays reflecting off of every material possible. A beam was precisely aimed at the face of Sicily while she slept sitting up against the wall. The heat had settled with enough friction to warm her skin to an abrupt awakening. Sicily squinted heavily at the hot heat waves that brushed against her. She let out a brisk yawn to stretch from her late night nap.

She was the only one awake to her amazement since she was a heavy sleeper. On an average day she would have been the last one to awake. This day was a reckoning of its own for Sicily. To her arise, she noticed her fellow scholars fast at sleep. It would have been tempting to wake them both up while she had gained control of her senses.

More or less Sicily sought toward another path in her mind. To herself she had agreed to check closely to what was taking place within the sanctuary. She searched each room by room with any
~~~

hope that nothing would be out of place or anyone harmed.

As much as she had hoped for the best she was gratefully unprovoked. Each unattended room was just as emptied as it had been the night before. In the kitchen she walks into a room that a slim figured white hair creature had lashed out at her.

Terrified, she screamed a loud high pitch yelp that echoed throughout the sanctuary. The continuous yell had reached the room of the scholars as she ran through the halls of the sanctuary. In a heat of alarm the scholars had all awakened worried to the dismay of something bad taking place and they were right unfortunately. Sicily had reached the priestess room when Buckner had been standing at the room's entrance. She ran into his arms and squeezed him as tight as possible.

"I'm happy to see that you are safe too Sicily. But what is wrong? "Buckner asked.

The range of scholars all had ran to the entrance of the priestess room. All of them were a bit more worried than they would've been suspected of being. The oldest scholar, Brett, was the first to make a comment as his role of leadership among the group.

His views were furious in comparison toward Cash, Buckner and the rest of the scholars. Everyone felt his nature to be too demanding, mainly toward any type of reasonable explanation.

"So what's all the noise about?" Brett demanded.

Sicily was rubbing the tears from her eyes while everyone was giving her wide stares. She felt speechless to those that came to her sight. Apparently she wasn't as strong as she hoped to being. Her response came out soft and frightful to the scholars.

"Well, something strange had jumped out of one of the closets in the kitchen, then I took off screaming. I'm sorry everyone I was so terrified. I could have died or been hurt for that matter." Sicily said.

"Well now that everyone is up. I would say that we go find out what is going on in the kitchen!" Brett stated.

Everyone followed as Brett broke the crowd to lead the masses to the kitchen. Even a very tired Cash had followed behind everyone in curiosity as to the culprit. Claps sounded from the shoes of the group marching toward the kitchen in search of this thing. Inside of the kitchen entrance gave a full laid out view of the room where the open closet could be seen.

"See, it came from over there where the door is open. The thing had long spaghetti white hair and long sharp teeth that looked like fangs. It was ferocious and creepy and I didn't know what to do about it." Sicily said while letting out a whimper.

Brett walked over to the closet to examine the truth of what she had said. He figured that at least a clue would lead him to something conclusive. The surroundings of the open door couldn't be seen at the entrance way. It laid hidden behind a large countertop that closed off the view of the closet area. The walk was short though, broken by the island shaped countertop.

Brett managed getting around the obstacles and setting up in front of the open door. The display upon his face was much like a ghost that was shocked. Others stranded to see around him to get a good view though they became just as shocked.

"Is this the white spaghetti haired, long fanged beast that lunged out at you." Brett said pointing at the mop. "I can't believe that this was going to take a chunk of your body."

A few of the scholars laughed while the others held onto their concerns for Sicily. Everyone at the same view where shocked to see nothing happened. Could she have made up the story in order to gain more attention? Only Sicily could've known and she was very upset that nobody had believed her. Why would she lie about something like that to anyone?

Now wasn't the time to be playing games and she knew that very well. As serious as she usually is then why would she change her attitude overnight like that? Sicily never wanted to be seen as a joke and she never will! this was odd for her.

"Could you try to pay more attention of what you are doing around here? Oh and guess what, you just volunteered to make breakfast. Alongside of Buckner and Cash that is. From here forth that's how we are going to get things done, guard duty then breakfast." Brett commented.

All the scholars followed Brett back to their room to prepare for the day. Cash, Buckner and Sicily all stayed in the kitchen to cook and clean. The pantry door was next to the open closet and Cash prepared himself to begin the cooking process.

"I'll help you clean this mess." Buckner stated.

Sicily gave an unsettled sigh of disbelief. She wanted to breakdown and pour out over her plight. She had already identified the truth and now everyone believes she is delusional. How could she win her worth if nobody would ever take her seriously?

"You know I saw what I said right?" Sicily stated.

Buckner picked up the mop and placed it back into the closet with the mop head flat on the floor. Some liquid cleanser laid wasted on the floor and Sicily had noticed it. Embedded in the mess was a single foot print that had faced away from the closet.

"Buckner." Sicily commented.

Buckner stopped what he was doing to turn to Sicily. As he began moving he nearly stepped with his right foot on the footprint. Sicily roared that he wouldn't do so as she attacked his foot.

"Look." Sicily commented.

She pointed to the foot print that was hidden inside of the puddled mess. She took notice that it was only one print and that it faced the opposite direction.

"Now do you believe me? "Sicily asked.

Buckner just stared in major disbelief. He was beginning to

understand that things were going to get way out of proportions. After noticing the print, they agreed on cleaning up the mess and worrying about the issue later. It didn't take too long for them to clean when they came to Cash.

Cash was already in the process of making breakfast for everyone else. He started by frying sausage, a piece for everyone and two slices of bread. An acceptable meal for everyone to get nourished and Cash was doing very well for the matter. On an average basis the meals were rationed to settle the stomach aches. The scholars always received just enough food to get by for the day.

"Okay, I'm frying up to twelve pieces of sausage at a time and I'll be done in no time." Cash states.

Sicily took a glance at Buckner as if she wanted him to tell Cash of the news. Together they wondered what would become of the Sanctuary if this thing was loose within it. Sicily didn't want to have anything to do with it from her personal stand point. The fact only remained for her that she would have to interact upon will for the safety of the sanctuary.

"Well don't get too excited there, Second in Command." Buckner commented. "We actually have found something very questionable that we think you might want to hear."

The meat that cash was frying was fully cooked and ready to be taken off the heat. As he did cash placed the frying pan onto a wooden block for it to cool off of. The meat still steered on the hot pan, so he had to stir them to keep them from burning.

"So what's up? The meats about done and I have time to listen some." Cash said.

"Alright listen well then. Something is in the Sanctuary and we don't know what it is, or where it could be." Buckner stated.

Cash had dropped his jaw in the mist of the confusion of what's going on. His eyes bulged before he spoke and he directed his thoughts openly.

"So let me get this straight. Something is within the sanctuary and you don't know what it is. Please tell me how you may be thinking that when all that was in the closet was the mop falling out!" Cash commented.

Sicily stepped to Cash and placed her hands upon his shoulder. She wanted to install her sincerity to him for his level of disbelief. The last thing that she wanted was for everyone not to believe anything that she'll say.

"Listen to me, please listen. We found some hard evidence to prove this and we need you to take our word on this one. I'm telling you Cash, would I ever lie to you about something this important?" Sicily stated.

Cash had to recall Sicily and how she's always direct on topics when it comes to typical things. She never voiced a negative opinion or had she ever joked in any regular accordance. Why couldn't he take her for something serious and not as an antic? Even though he couldn't allow them to notice it, Cash was beginning to feel weary about how this was going to play out. Cash made sure he was going to finish with the food while Buckner and Sicily tended to the search for the mysterious being.

~ ~ ~

After getting drunk for the night, the dark priest was enjoying great sleep when he finally came to. The morning sunlight beamed through the slits in his blinds causing a brick scope of lighting flowing into his room. He must have slept for hours within the morning time. Action, action, action had ran repetitively through his mind. It was time for another goal to be set into place so that he may bury his anguish. At the current moment he didn't actually come to the full conclusion as to when, where or how he would fulfill the onset of his ministries. Like any greater measure of thought the priest took into account that he needed two things at the least. One was for more scholars to become future priest and priestess and the time to rebuild the foyer.

"Time, this will be essential to me." Samhain implied.

He stood firmly looking out of the window in a shear gaze at the few people that walked around. The majority of them were older people who attended to odd jobs for a regular days earning. Senselessly he knew better then to try any of them for any of the positions available. He needed youths with great physical attributes to implore his services. A mid to older twenty year old would do fine to carry on the priesthood.

Time had daunted him more as he managed to consider and reconsider his options in trying to overtake the small city. It may be viable to him for an extended force of expendable assets yet he questioned how he could subject them all in just one solid interaction. It would be easily done with the range of strength that is offered by the ancient orbs would magnify that ability in theory. With enough orbs being well placed throughout the corners of the city he then could force the high rule of his takeover. Step by step the ideas rolled into his mind within each hour of the day.

Samhain grew unsettled by worrying of his plan of action. He built up an urge to want to eat and drink while the time forged onward. From his coat he grabbed a cloth pouch that contained all of his coins to pay for his serviceable needs. He placed the cloth into one of his pockets before leaving out of his room. The walk to the restaurant was short though it left him undetermined to think about how to view the people that were downstairs.

The saloon was open and partially filled with people from one side of the bar to the other. The few filled tables ran card games and had glasses of beer to fuel the idol ego. Samhain was aware of the nature of those types of individuals who were runners that are restless in chasing their financial statures. Those type of people that sought more for gain by any means necessary type. Charmers like them would cause distress anytime and anywhere their insatiable quench grew.

It wouldn't been in his nature to confront them without having to deal with a greater means of resistance from the remaining consort. Samhain took more time to gather in his stakes by sorting through the few people in his head. Old, young and maimed people were all around him to an relentless extent. A good drink and meal would settle his resolve for finding his next mark for now. The priest set in at the bar to make his order of fresh fried ham slapped on two pieces of rye bread.

"Will that be all for you honey?" the owner asked him.

Samhain took his coin pouch and withdrew a few coins to settle up his order. He kept the coins in his hand and shook them as it rattled in his hand. They rattled and clicked with ease in his hand like a chime in the wind.

"I will also take a drink of cider as well, if I may." Samhain impressed.

He placed the money onto the countertop and waited for a response from the owner. She gave him a quick look then proceeded with taking the money form the countertop.

"How about your change?" the owner asked.

Samhain waived the woman off without any declarative suggestion. He wasn't focused on the money as much as he was looking to salvage his ministry. More people began to enter the bar that included a blonde and a man that was slightly taller than her. They sat with each other as if they had been a couple who knew each other very well.

Out of every conversation topic that has come up, the woman exemplified in his observation as a great conversationalist. The fire, in her eyes, was lit like a glowing candle that shined in the darkest room. She smiled very elegantly. Her teeth showed a beautiful pearl white gleam that sparkled within the loom. Even though her face was very pale and her noise was narrow, like witches, she was very beautiful in detail. Her eyes where cocked in a cat like ridge that promulgate her blue eyes.

The woman was magnificent to look at and the man was handsome to his sort, his height covered over his masculine body structure that fitted him well in comparison to everyone else around the pair stood out quite strikingly. Persuasively they carried a grade of purity that relished their glow. Happily they walked as if love had moved them spuriously.

Together the two lit up the gloomy room that exemplified a seed of darkness. Samhain was the most evident in spotting out a difference in other individuals. It was clear to him that everyone had carried a certain graveness about themselves. A skill that set his value to an unrivaled magnitude compared to anyone else. For any understanding he knew that the people where real about who they were and what they believed.

Samhain gave the two people a good stare down as he watched them move around the room. They spoke openly and freely to everyone within the room as if they were one of them. Of them, as if it was a purpose to them to encourage and enlighten others with hopes and dreams. In the beamed eyes of Samhain they were the small town. To everyone else a small fraction of joy had curved over them as if angels had carried them around.

The man walked into the back storage room of the bar area.

He stayed away for a moment's time yet Samhain kept a close eye to him. Within each moments gaze he had settled his thoughts to their accords. How was it that they have forgone the regular challenges that everyone else had succumbed to? Outside of the pair everyone else was staggered with despair, envy, and even for some, hatred.

Samhain was a priest yet not the same division of a natural priest, by means that he was tried, only by his use of the satanic art, of animal sacrifice and demonic magic. Regular priest had told him that his heart was greater for good and that they acknowledged his stems for being visionary. The love of his inner viewing of everyone was his greatest adornment. Without further agreement his priesthood was his alone to the basis of his powers.

A quick sip of his glass had tickled his mind with more equitable thoughts. If it would be any easier for him then he could convert the town, with the grade of potent concerns that rushed over the hearts of the purest individuals throughout the city. Greatness had been reached in his mind and he knew well why. He was a priest that has been labeled dark, though within him was purity.

The priest's advantage to others wasn't his design to overtake or rob them of life. Instead he was a leader of ancient biblical proportions that was to revive the people of life to overcome the misinformation of God. He was far from the antichrist, by the truth of him he was pro Christ by design and education. To him by being an only source, was he ever denied by the known groupings of the lending churches and their followers? Sacrifices offered by his hands had encouraged sustainment to God, gratifying the everlasting life of humanity.

The priest guzzled down another gulp of his glass as he kept an eye on the way his drink bubbled. He was infatuated with its designs of minute bubbles and golden color. It reminded him of the early morning sunrise and how it conducted time. He knows well that time is to be challenged at one point of life. Though he understands that the sunrise will still be an element of more time!

For Samhain his views, goals and tribulations will be ongoing for years to follow. His mind is forged against the accolades of the demons to come. With enough hope he would be prepared for anything that will soon ensue. The morning light was an adaptive inverse to him as it is. Brighter than any star, the sun was the dilution to the most sectioned beast to ever roam the earth.

His tactics were scaled as limitless, though he needed more than an array of tactful skills. Samhain needed more diverse leaders to take up for his cause with his sanctuary. Yet who of all of the people within the world would him chose, or evenly the ones within the small town? The strains of residual strengths have made Samhain overlook the people on the bar. The youthful male that walked in would have made an excellent candidate to the acceptation.

The woman that the male had coupled with was spending time conversing with the owner, however the dark priest wasn't known for reading lips.

His only exception was when he could tell that the rate of translation was diverse and appealing to the both of them. Upon exchanging words the two had laughed wholeheartedly. It seemed that the young woman had a knack for speaking. He noticed the two women shaking hands and giving praises unto one another.

Right then it wasn't too clear to him what had transpired until the owner had welcomed the woman behind the bar. She was being offered a job from what it seemed as the lady began serving customers. Samhain couldn't resist keeping an eye upon the young lady. He assured himself, that she would become an excellent priestess within his sanctuary. Her great use of words would prove well in lectures to the peers.

The young man had entered the bar area of the saloon. He wore a heavy set of gloves that would protect his fist upon creating impacts against objects. The suggestion had come to him that the man was possibly the bouncer of the saloon. His gloves and heavy build had given him that impression. The man took up a discussion with the owner before he finally retreated to the door. It was all clear after that as he knew what the man was.

The two youthful adversaries, who would prove great in his sanctuary, were among him. Without the trial of Maxin the priest wouldn't have even considered of recruitment. It would seem that the two were without question of consideration to him. The lady walked over to him on the opposite side of the bar with suggestions to drink. She gazed heavily into Samhain's pale face to drive her concerns. Without much resistance he considered another drink as he untied a solid coin.

"Maybe I would be able to buy you one sometime when your shift is over." Samhain said.

He bared his thoughts more frankly and was open with no real intent to flirt with the woman. His goal was to open her into discussion to further review her as a candidate. Samhain wanted to know if she could deliver more bang for what she could do so easily. Upon analyzing each other the lady gave a nice smile. Her face cringed before she spoke, so Samhain gathered his conclusion before she had returned to work.

"Well that would depend if my fiancé would appreciate us sitting together." The lady responds.

Undoubtedly, Samhain wasn't hurt by her sincere concern of her relationship. It was the use of the woman that had toppled his thoughts. How could he find the time to pull her to his sanctuary and begin new studies? 'Soon,' he concluded to his thoughts, 'soon' to him having his way and restructuring his founded sanctuary.

Samhain chugged a few gulps of his drink while he kept a watchful eye on the two youthful adults. He would mold them into becoming a part of his faction, he imagined the acts that he would use for them to subdue to his bidding. Another sip of his drink before his gazes had faded black like an isolated room with no lighting. The priest drunk too much and was ready for a rest. Sounds of his head slamming against the bar table had startled the other customers in an instant.

The sound had alarmed the youthful bouncer who had

stepped to Samhain's side. Immediately he checked the priest vitals to see if he had suffered a heart attack. Assured he knew that the man had only passed out due to his consistent heartbeat.

"Excuse me, but does this man have a room here? I think he's going to be out for a while." The man said.

Behind the bar was a chart with room numbers on them and a name to the room. The man looked over the chart to where the owner had pointed to.

"Samhain," the man implied as he examined the room number.

"Yup, you should hurry along because he looks like he could use the rest," The owner suggested.

The young man was appeased by the way she had addressed him. He was even more overtaken by the massive size of the sleeping man. His room was on the second floor and the flight of stairs was an extreme case to carry a person larger than his own size.

"Hey, sis." The man opened up. "You think you can help me get him up the stairs."

The lady gave him a wild look as if he had been demented. Her body frame wasn't anywhere close to the same standards of men and she didn't really want to overextend her own muscles. As far the bond that she carried with her brother, the bouncer, she wasn't in an optioned moment. Their relationship was a real give and take with one another and it's what led them to getting ahead in life. She gave a low sigh before wiping her hands upon a dry towel.

"Alright, Chief, I gotcha." She replied.

She walked over and gave her shoulder for support. Samhain's body was lifeless and far heavier by comparison. Without his use of his muscle he was just more dead weight. She pulled at his arm that flailed without life that rested on her shoulder. His body was heavy on her since she was slightly shorter than her brother.

"Can you handle him?" The man asked.

The young lady suppressed her feelings and gave a white lie. Either way she was needed to help out.

"I got this, we can go forward." She replied.

~ ~ ~

The sizzling of the sausage being cooked sounded loudly in a high pitched whistle. Cash finished the last few pieces of meat. Reluctantly, he whipped a large pot of cream of wheat for extra filling to anyone that felt very hungry. He managed good use of his cooking skills that he'd developed over time. "Now we can see what's wrong." Cash proclaimed to himself. "Come and get it!" He roared out.

The young adult stacked handfuls of plates on the countertop as well as silverware. He did it just before leaving the kitchen in his search for Buckner and Sicily. The younger scholars brushed past him in a heightened swiftness as the older ones walked briskly.

"See, this is why you were chosen first. I already knew that I could count on you. So what I want to do is try this for every two weeks or until Samhain returns at least. You can handle that right, or am I asking for too much?" Brett asked.

Cash stared heavily toward the scholar and into his black eyes. He hadn't spent too much time talking to the scholar and he didn't even know his name. All that he'd realized was that he pays attention and that he's been around for some time before him. At the end of the debate about trust or even respect, in Cash's eyes he had it.

"You know what? We're all good." Cash said at the breaking of a handshake. "What's your name anyway? It took this for me to ask, but here it goes."

"Brett." The scholar responded with pride, "time to eat."

Both scholars parted ways, Brett headed to the kitchen as Cash searched for the others. He really was clueless about where to find them and the sanctuary was expansive. Surely he continued walking through the hall in hopes to find something out.

"What do you think it was that was hiding in the kitchen pantry? Perhaps a ghost that was hidden in the sanctuary somewhere and it's trying to disturb everyone whenever it gets ready to!" Buckner asked.

"Ha," Sicily chuckled. "Strangely enough that thing wasn't any ghost. If you ask me it was something more. I mean it's hair was too organic, it's eyes practically glowed in the dark and it had very sharp teeth on it. If I knew any better I would say that ghost don't carry those types of features on them."

Buckner implied, "Wow, I guess you do make a valid point, but what the heck are we even up against right now? Whatever it is it couldn't haven't appeared out of nowhere. This thing has to been around for some time. But the most shocking question is why we weren't ever notified about this before?"

"You know that's an exceptional truth Buckner. The priesthood hasn't been too honest with us for some time now, huh? I mean, we wouldn't be so sheltered if there wasn't something to hide from." Sicily commented.

"Right, right, and right. How long do you think Samhain is going to be gone? Things aren't exactly going to be the same without him around you know. We might have to do everything under the wings of that older scholar." Buckner stated.

"Oh, you mean Brett. Yeah he's not so bad once you spend some time with him. He's like a kid in heart except that he's more mature than everyone else." Sicily said while trying to be insightful.

Sicily took a second to try to gather her thoughts together, for any reason she would stare out into nothing. Her definition for doing so was to gather more insight from her surroundings or even what she could think of. Cash stuck on her mind as she tried to question the reasons why he hasn't decided on taking the lead. He was always the first scholar to participate in any open activities, yet nobody figured him as being the most potential. Sicily's emotions for Cash were leaving her open and the others were beginning to tell.

"Um earth to Sicily. What kind of thing are taking you away from us at this moment because I seem to remember that when you get like this you seem to be a bit in a deep probing trance that drives your questions over the top." Buckner implied.

Cash forwarded his mind back and forth between them as he approached them. He was always aware of her trances, yet he didn't want to bother her questioning which direction she had in opposing whether or not if she would bark his ear off from an upsetting thought. If she wants to speak on it then she would. It was just how she was at that type of moment.

Slowly Sicily drew her head to face both of the male scholars. Widely she opened her eyes to give them shattered looks that she didn't want to express her thoughts. Surely her preferences toward Cash would prove to be more apparent as she stands firmly toward his side.

"I'm sorry. I think I'm just thrown off by what is happening. I couldn't imagine that we are now faced with a more opposing threat other than the feral dogs. I mean we grew up here and they were the only danger that I have ever known. Now that all of the leaders are all gone, we really don't have much support to take us to our highest level of defense." Sicily stated.

In general she was right about how much impact it was going to take to maintain against this new unknown threat. The situation is very sensitive on many grounds as Buckner and Cash began delivering more into the situation.

"Hey I think we should really start searching for this thing," Cash said.

"We could have problems of trying to track it down after nightfall." Sicily commented.

"Makes sense to me," Buckner replied.

Even though he wasn't the best of scholars he carried a strong sense of leadership skills that his close companions had valued about him. Sicily was well to follow him ever since Buckner had rescued her from a pack of wild dogs. The way he stepped in had encouraged her strongly to stay on his side.

"So how are we going to do this?" Sicily asked.

She gave a fierce look at Buckner before turning back toward Cash. The female firmly gripped her knuckles in a clench to drive home her immediate anger. Sicily wasn't the type to give up too easily and she knew that this wasn't going to become that time either.

"Well for one the kitchen is all checked out and it is safe to check a listing of possible options." Cash said.

"Okay, let's check the cellar first since everyone else is upstairs. Maybe we can be able to catch a break that way." Sicily suggested.

"Sounds good," Buckner replied.

"Yeah, let's do this." Cash replied.

The group all turned in unison in a side by side walk toward the hall. The action was much anticipated by the group. They had all these cards on the line, the priesthood, their futures, their lives. There was no turning back for them.

~~~

The scrolling sun began dissipating within the horizon as the last of the sun rays peeped through the closed window. The air had thickened from the reign of temperature that caused Samhain to awaken with a sweltering amount of sweat that moistened his body. His mouth was heavy and dry that caused him to smack his lips together as he searched for more moisture. By the time that he had passed out he began realizing that he slept with every piece of clothing still on his body. The heavy trench coat had weighed on his body as he raised himself from his rested position.

His mind was disoriented from the high amount of alcohol that he had drunk from hours before. The man's eyes felt as if they had been rubbed continuously as the daze in his eyes lasted for a few minutes after waking. The empty room looked as if it was larger than it had been since he last saw it the day before. Checking to see if anything was missing, he remembered that all of his possessions were on him except for the clothes that he had cleaned. They lay in a chair neatly folded as if had reminded him that his mission wasn't yet completed.
~~~

"What will become of all of this?" The priest had thought out loud to himself. He finished rising from his mattress in a search for a lantern to get enough light to scavenge through his pocket change. He needed a full look at what he had for incase of a manageable escape. The wealthy priest would usually carry an abundance of a few grand on any regular stroll from the sanctuary. He had to remember the countless purchases that he recently made in order to make things more comfortable for the priesthood.

Fifteen shillings he had spent and had his thoughts had been filled with idea of making another sanctuary within the town. He began claiming reasons to how he'll convince some more people to start the cause. After a quick wash up he bundled his clothes to pay for them to be washed. The tavern was filled with plenty of people for him to stake a claim, except he wasn't prepared yet to consume them from their regular activities.

One thing was certain and that was the fact that he could easily cause a rapt from just changing the elements of the environment around them. A quick stroll through the grouping of people and he could tell a difference from a change in their pace of activities. It would then become easy for him to be singled out from the starred sets of individuals. A few eyes had come back onto him as the people watched him in his stroll. The gazes nearly crippled him with the thought that he might be had.

Without allowing anything to break him from a forward jolt, he rushed for an empty round table that was in the far corner of the tavern. It was a good way for him to have the atmosphere to drag into his presence. The many onlookers turned from settling in on him as they withdrew gazes. For Samhain it was a chance for him to find a whole within the ranks.

The 'whom' could never have come in a faster form as he watched a young male leave the bar after speaking with the bartender. Everyone else on the other hand, they all were tied up into a stream of countless interactions.

"Check," Samhain expressed himself.

The priest created a draw for him to leave and mend his services from the young fit male. Elegantly he left without question from anyone within the bar. In an enraged rush he turned in his scouting for the young male. It was just beyond the road past a view over his right shoulder that he saw the young man. He walked swiftly before him yet the man was still close enough to be met by him.

Samhain took a smooth stride with his hat tilted downward alongside of his face to block himself from being fully recognizable. He started counting to himself the number of paces that it was taking him to finally reach up to the adolescent. Forty five, forty six… he continued counting as endlessly as the numbers had begun to increase. He came as close as he could to the young man when he turned around at a face to face stare.

"Excuse me, do you want something?" the young man asked.

Samhain began to speak before he'd notice a glare coming from a tree within the distance. With a quick glance back into the young man's eyes, he beamed a sharp gesture.

"Once you take a step you will become short with memory." Samhain forcefully yielded his trance.

The young man was concerned that he had begun speaking to this man and that he oddly said what he had. Within no time Samhain turned away as swiftly as he had taken to get there. The young man gave a dumb founded stare at the fact that he had just seen this man. Dauntingly the glaring eyes from the tree had stretched into a deep pause gaze upon the back of the young man.

The yellow glowing eyes watched the young man turn to only notice that he stopped moving. The eyes fluttered in all its amazement to actively realize that there was a subject for consumption. The pair of eyes stroked the tree branches in a downward fall. Inactively the eyes had erupted with a massive body that was covered with fur. The beastly creature was a feral, one of the wolf creatures that roamed for blood.

The dazed man wasn't prepared for what was at his approach. The saliva from the mouth of the large beast had dribbled across the rough rigged oversized teeth of the creature. The young man was unaware of anything that was going on around him. His mind had gone blank, as to having no clue to his plan of actions. Snarls rolled and ringed from the open mouth of the feral.

At once it was enough to draw back the attention of the dazed man whom grew to shock. The approach of the feral had caused the young man to run in a swift trot through a yard that was by his side. The shadowed field was ruined with numerous trees that held very little light within the groups. Branches swung in and the young man fled, making his way through the rough mounds of branches. A look behind himself he didn't see much, yet his hearing was adequate enough to hear the rustling noise from the trees that were above and around him.

Crack, a noise sounded.

A tree branch had fallen to the left side of the young man. The loud crash had startled him so much, that he began sprinting immediately. As fearful as the man was, he didn't notice that oversized wolf that kept foot behind him. Both the young fit male and the wolf huffed and wheezed for breath to enter them as they ran.

Even as the young man was short with memory, he knew well that shelter would be his best option for his protection. The horde of trees was coming to an end as the young man noticed a light that sat on the side of a building through the distance. Fear ran in an immense amount as the man felt a claw dig through his right shoulder.

"Argh!" The young male roared loudly.

He knew that it would have been seconds more that the creature would've been able to reach him. It was at that moment when he drew a plucking knife from his pocket. It was a gardening tool that he used on a regular basis. The swinging knife tore halfway through the finger of the beast. Blood rushed heavily from the open wound of the creature as it further ran down the young man's back.

The beast whimpered as it slowed in momentum while the young man continued forward. The base end of the row of trees had opened up to the young man as he reached a barn house that cased the light that he once had seen as he ran. There wasn't much else in the range of sight but open fields for the farmer's crops. Within the distance of the man he was able to enter into the barn as the wide door had swung open. As he entered the barn he forced the door shut behind him.

The man gasped trying to inhale air within his lungs as he viewed the inside of the large scaled barn. Right next to a window laid a stack of chicken coops that housed dozens of chickens. They all chirped at the crashing sounds that the man had made once startling them. The clucking noises didn't disturb the man as much as the claw mark that was deep into his back.

Blood still rushed heavily from his shoulder as the man tried to contain the leaking of red blood that flowed from the wound. He sat on a hay stack and tore his shirt to bandage it. There wasn't anything around to clean it with so he didn't bother to try. Everything had happened so suddenly and it was leaving him numb. The man trembled for minutes before he began coming back to his regular composure.

Helplessly he tried to gaze upon the chickens that clucked before noticing a dark shadow that appeared past the window. The dark figure burst forward in an endless rage breaking the glass. Glass shards flew onto and beyond the chicken cages and right past the young man. The wide cages rattled that the beast could not get past them. Revoltingly he stretched a pair of wires to opening as it snatched one of the chickens from the coop.

Feathers rustled as the chicken clucked from being snatched from the cage. A smoky haze had flourished the barn house that gave no clear sight to where the large best could have maneuvered itself. It had seemed that the young gardener wasn't the only one that was a bit fearful. Inside of the birdcage, feathers rustled as the chickens began to climb on top of one another in a struck rage to hide from the frolicking beast.

Blood rushed from the man's shoulder in a smothered rush of flush red ooze. The remaining sleeve of the man's shirt draped from his shoulder.

Skkirt, the sound of fabric tearing echoed loudly inside of the empty barn. The man shook in pain from the shirts pressure upon his shoulder. He knew that he'll lose consciousness unless he immediately tie up his wound better and with more pressure.

"Aargh," he yelped as his eyes began to roll to the back of his head. The young man's sight had begun to blur and the sound of clucking chicken had rustled in his ear before passing out.

~ ~ ~

Darkness had consumed the stairwell and beveled hall that led way into the cellar. It would've been very risky if that the bunch couldn't conceive light as they stepped a little further.

"Wait!" Sicily whispered.

"For what, were almost there!" Cash responded.

"Right but we can't see anything either genius. We need this…"

Sicily drew her sword as she unplugged the handle that contained a shard of glass like crystal. Her left hand was free and the end of the handle hung by cords of thread that she wrapped around her right wrist.

"Illuminous." She chanted.

The crystal glowed like a lantern that spread throughout the staircase, thus giving reflected light to every glass piece in sight. The cellar in full was radiated by a light blue glow that filled the grounds bottom. As excited as the two males had been it was shortly lived to see a strange figure that stood before them. Buckner reached for Sicily pulling her closer to him as he poured out. "Come here."

The sight was full of discouragement to see the being that held no remnants for a full functioning person. Instead it was easy to tell that the being was a ghost of some sort, with an ability to pressure reality with forceful presence. The feet of the ghost had never touched the stairwell. It was easy to see that it was between the steps in full. The ghost looked like a young girl, which was frail with long hair.

"Please don't scare me," the female ghost cried out. "I don't like it when you cast that light on me. It harms me and I'm already dead."

"Did you all hear that?" Sicily asked.

"You hurt her with the light." Cash said.

Sicily withdrew the light by covering it into her armpit, so that the light was shining behind her.

"Why are you scaring us?" Buckner questioned. "What have we done to you?"

"Nothing… yet the big ones try to banish me and it only hurts when they wield the light," the girl proclaimed.

The group gave each other a wide-eyed gaze over, wondering who the girl was suggesting about.

"It would be almost safe to say that we don't have anything to worry about." Sicily suggested.

"Almost would take the merit for that idea but we don't want it to turn around on us." Buckner stated.

"But maybe she'll be able to tell us what's going on outside of the priesthood. Even better what's going on here?" Sicily commented.

Nobody knew how close to the truth she could be. What had gone on outside of the priesthood and why had the girl been a secret for so long. It would be easy to say that the priest had been trying to protect them but who would actually know who's to say so.

"What is your name?" Sicily turned to ask without shining the light too brightly toward the floating ghost.

"Alana," the female ghost replied without freight. "I used to stay in this area with my family. It was years ago that I would wonder around and spend my time playing with my friends. Until one night in October a man had come into town and asked if he could start a religion. My family hasn't believed in higher powers so we didn't take any interest. As the days passed everyone was talking about him and what they began to believe about his thoughts and teachings. I remember someone saying that he said he believes in Christ yet he follows a higher being than him."

Sicily gave Alana a good look over to try to analyze her. Faintly the girl still had clothes, or at least they favored clothes and that she wasn't naked. Why would a ghost have clothes for any reason, maybe it was the mentioning of respect for the dead? It would've been rude for a naked spirit to roam without any self-respect to be covered up. Her clothes weren't ragged except for three tears upon her collar.

In the eyes of Sicily she had never seen or spoke to a spirit before, yet she would applaud that the girl didn't seem to be of a poor background. As common as she stood the young girl had favored wealth at its most and was a child of the instance. Figuring the girl was well to do but why had she died such an untiring death to begin with. The question seeped into Sicily's mind during the greeting and then showed in her work in asking. Yet before she did

Sicily noticed the scar to the side of the girl's neck.

It would be easy to say that the tear in her clothes had settled well with the one to her neck and was the possible source of death.

"I'm curious," Sicily stated.

Alana gazed deeply into Sicily's eyes as her own had darkened in the shaded stairwell.

"What might that be?" Alana responded.

Sicily gestured with her hand toward the open land around her. "You said you were from around here, once the sanctuary had started right?" she asked.

"That's right around ten years earlier perhaps, around the same time that the governance was becoming stronger. Why do you ask me so?" Alana asked.

"Curiously, you've been around here but this is the first time that we've seen or heard from you. Why is that?" Sicily questioned.

"Easy, I was trapped here in the basement, making it my tomb of a home to dwell in. Nothing could keep me from leaving because of the spells that kept me trapped by the harness of light. Someone didn't want me to wander around so easily as I'm capable of doing. But I see that all that is different now since the large one is now hurt." Alana said.

"Hugh," Sicily gasped, "you mean the warrior priest, he was recently hurt with wounds like yours."

"Without his light spells to contain me, I've been freed for all to see." Alana stated.

"Sure but you can't go around to bother people it would be terrible for the public to endure." Sicily stated.

"But there is something that I need from other beings, it's only my loneliness at times. I hear you all laughing over the years and I wanted to see you once the spells had stopped. I hid in the pantry to keep myself from being seen but I guess that didn't work too well. Well enough that I frightened you and I came back here to hide." Alana said.

"Alright, everything is fine now since your reasoning to us. And then the others…" Sicily was shut off.

"The others might not take the time to figure me out as you are they might even try to kill me or banish me once again." Alana blurted.

"We get your point," Buckner states.

"Then what difference would we be to you?" Cash asked.

"I thought we were becoming friends, since you didn't want to harm me. Understanding is what I need from you. I need you to understand, the person I am." Alana states.

"You know what happened to you?" Cash asked.

Alana began to whimper after she looked away for more sympathy. Cash's words were eminent, sharp and intangible to her feelings.

"Sorry if you don't want to answer me!" Cash stated.

"It's alright." Alana replied looking at the three. "It was roughly ten years past since the incident anyway, I just thought I was past it all."

"It all, you say that like it was a massacre!" Buckner replied.

Alana didn't want to turn shade from her mood so she didn't rush to answer Buckner's statement. After turning away she gave a harsh look before she answered.

~ ~ ~

The walk through the small city was short but gruesome to a lonely mind. Samhain couldn't wait to reunite at his home. The time it took for him to become involved toward his lesson plans with the students was enough to encode grief. Shadows quarreled in the night as he approached the end of the city limits and to a bridge. A foul stench reached his nose at the peak of the bridge that made him think twice upon passing.

Between the smell that was foul he kindled the taste of fresh bread that he had nearly seen a few homes back from which he had come. "A nice meal would serve this quest. A few more nights then it's back to home." Samhain said aloud.

The priest began to travel back south to his home at the bar. He didn't want to bother himself with questions that he alone can't answer. The fresh aroma of bread watered his mouth as mounds of saliva filled his glands. Fresh warm soup and bread would cause his hunger to stop with a late meal. A pair of feuding eyes had followed the priest in search of warmth to feed his belly.

The path trailed a few more feet before intersecting at a home that lay away from the bridge toward the city. As Samhain walked the pair of eyes had scaled through the darkness in an attempt to catch up to him. The air had turned frigid and almost alarming cold with slough. It had become a worrisome feeling for Samhain that he hadn't even caught notice of the trailing creature that lurked. The change in the atmosphere had moved a cursor within his mind to pick up his pace.

The wind hissed horribly as the air scolded the priest with might. The eyes of the priest rolled around in concerns to the change of atmosphere. He knew well that for any possibility of something going wrong it would. A howl had rushed in the distant air that had set alarm to the priest and the lurking creature at bay. As wondrous as it is, neither one could yield to the howling sound of a praying wolf or two. The following eyes had backed away from Samhain in a forceful retreat and Samhain was on a brisk walk home.

People began talking about the people who were in the quiet town and Samhain had come in under the radar. Nobody wanted to take the time to speak to him or to figure him out. For all they had known he was a part of the small group that was just moving into the town. It wasn't until when Samhain had entered back into the lodge that the towns people talking had turned small. It wasn't every day that a person would allow a complete stranger into their lives in an instant.

Throughout all the glances coming from everyone Samhain managed to avoid any real conversations before sitting back at the bar. From the side of the window he can see a person staring into the window. He felt he should not to relinquish any idea to the person before he began ordering his soup and bread. It wasn't long before two men in trench coats had appeared as they trapped him in at his seat.

"We've been looking for you." The man to Samhain's left had spoken.

"It's not every day that a priest such as oneself would fulfill the oracle of time." The man to Samhain's right had presented.

"The oracle of time is a kook and should never be believed." Samhain replied.

"Well we believe that you will submit to us, because of what we will show you. Believe me a priest such as me would never cheat the oracle." The man to Samhain's left implied.

Frustration had begun to bury within Samhain as he wished he could stir the minds of the two priests but nothing would stand. The fathom priest had known that all too well.

"My meal is almost ready, I shall have a bite before we make any end meetings." Samhain stated.

"And we shall do that all too well my priest." The other

priest spoke.

~ ~ ~

The scholars had finished speaking to Alana and found out that she was a preeminent to the family of the politician Jasper. They stayed in Central for years as their family had passed down the traditions of governance. One in which her father was running for. Mind you it was before her family's untimely destruction. They came to understand each other very well and in how the scholars were all looking to better their own lives if they could. The process of getting to know each other became short when Sicily had ended the conversation to get back to the others.

At the head of the steps the door creaked as the door opened. The scholars were speechless with one another as they came to the top of the steps. They began to hear howls throughout the halls and outside. Closing the door Sicily runs into a frightening haul as she screams. Her heart pumped with a racing degree of in-explainable fear that swallowed her chest.

"What are all of you doing up this late. You know it's time for rest within these hours." Words filled through the air like a sharp knife through water. The words of Nattuck crackled the cheer within the scholars.

"I left for a short while to return to chaos in the school. What has gone on here?" Nattuck demanded.

The scholars were short of comforting words to stretch out the explanations to Nattuck, and his desire to understand the last few hours of time. It was as if they all knew very well that if they spoke they wouldn't be understood.

"We all wanted to await your return," Cash stated.

"Right." Sicily responds.

"So much that we all wanted to stay up and we began training in the basement." Buckner adds on.

Nattuck gave a hard look before thinking to speak again. "All of you know that those quarters are off limits."

The scholar's nod their heads in unison, as they sigh for comfort. The priest reached for the door to close it behind the scholars. How much have they really seen, and could he begin to trust these youthful scholars?

"I will be sure to take a look around down there, perhaps anything could be missing." Nattuck said giving the scholars a wild look over. "For now it would be best that you all go get some rest."

The three took off without question! It really wasn't their best idea to spout comments that would expel them from the temple. It took them a minute for them to reach their quarters within the temple that they all walked very slowly. A cold chill had resonated furring their time together among the other scholars. A feeling so weird that Sicily knew she had to break through the ice.

"She liked me!" Sicily cried.

Buckner watched Cash try to silence Sicily before she awoke

the other scholars. He suggested that they would spawn from the fact that they held guard duty before Elee's turn with Maxin. Cheerily enough Sicily didn't want to squander to the comment, so in a softer tone she repeated, "She likes me!"

"Sure she does," Buckner replied.

"She liked all of us." Cash stated.

"I know but for a first encounter it wasn't a half bad experience!" Sicily implied.

Buckner and Cash chuckled, it excited them to see Sicily so excitedly.

"Maybe we can go back," Sicily said.

"Well…" Cash was cut off.

The sounds of aggressive talking had shut down his train of thought when he began listening to the voices.

"Shh," Cash demanded. "Something is going on."

Buckner and Sicily couldn't help but to listen to Cash as they followed him in his steps. They stroked the doorway of their quarters into the darkened hallway when a light burrowed from where Maxin and Elee had slept.

"Nattuck," Cash whispered. "Why is he yelling?"

"Let's see," Sicily suggested.

The three kept silent as they hugged the walls of the hallway toward Maxin's room. The darkness had made it harder to dodge the low hanging pictures that smacked Buckner as he walked.

"This is something that is never to be expected of a priest let alone a Celtic priest." Nattuck stated.

"This is nothing more than something bigger than the priesthood Nattuck," Elee responds. "This is bigger than mankind."

The three overheard the conversation, but couldn't grip to the whole arc of things. What was bigger than mankind and why had it unexpectedly made a change to the priesthood? Nobody was determined to ask as they honed in on the rest of the conversation.

"Then what is it to be expected," Nattuck asked. "How much more time does he need to fully heal."

"Good question," She responds," maybe he's not gonna heal at all. I've never seen anything like this before in my life and here we go dealing with this."

"Any brother of mine isn't dyeing on me; maybe we can try something else other than the rejuvenation spells. Of course it has to be something strong yet powerful enough to unbind his sickness." Nattuck explained.

"But there isn't anything. This man is anything but sick after what he's done to me and I feel funny for the time being." Elee stated.

"What if we use the orbs?" Nattuck continued.

Sicily pressed against the door a bit causing it to creak. The noise was so startling that Elee and Nattuck stopped talking.

"True enough if they'll work but we'll never know unless we have all six of them. We only contain two of them within the Sanctuary." Elee stated.

"That's true, our brothers in the far city will have the rest. First thing in the morning I will begin the search in the far city. I'm sure you'll be able to handle things around here." Nattuck trails.

The three scholars had heard it all, Maxins' sickness, the orbs, and Nattucks attempt to head out to the far city. What will all of this round off to and will it become way too much to handle. These thoughts had triggered the three scholars before they retreated back to add a positive end to the acquisition.

~ ~ ~

The bar had a private back room that becomes open to the public only by a request. The three priests entered the room alongside of Samhain's meal, to encourage his appetite. A large table stood in the middle of the room with four chairs to give rest to the gentlemen.

"Please don't hesitate to take a seat priest, the things that we are about to show you are major need to know information." The first priest said.

Samhain didn't take too long to heed to the priests suggestions as he sat down. His plate of fresh meat and two over easy eggs steamed with heat that would water the mouth of any on-comer. Samhain gave in to watching the two men who were close to one another in size. Both men stood at around six feet high with a large build to them. The talkative priest sat across from Samhain as the second priest stood readily, drawing an orb from his bag. Samhain had posed with a fork filled with food upon it aimed for his mouth.

"What is this about?" Samhain asks curiously. He gave a dark look to the two priest and wanted answers. Samhain recalled the words of the talkative priest about the oracle. With an orb on the table he began to understand how serious it could be.

"I haven't seen one of these since I found the two that turned up in a wolf's den." Samhain stated.

"Yes we know," the talkative priest comments. "That is why we came to you Samhain. With the powers of God I am allowed to see into the oracle and pull fragments of the future. From there the oracle had shown me the great danger of your sanctuary and what becomes of you at the face of two rivals beings that are a scale of chaos."

Samhain completely lost his appetite, pushing his bowl to the side. His eyes widened to following what the priest were telling him. He wanted to catch every detail about the corruption that is to consume him in the near future.

"So at this point how does all of this take place, THE DESTRUCTION OF MY SANCTURARY AND THE

COMING OF MY RIVALS?" Samhain asked.

The two priest gaze into each others brown eyes to focus on how they will reveal the level of detail that is being asked of them. "How will it come to surpass indeed," the two men clarified among each other. "That is why we spent the time coming here to look for you; to challenge you before it is too late to understand."

The priest that stood, looked as if he was younger and more vulgar than the other priest being able to control the elements of darker magic. To his side he carried a long sword as the first priest held strongly to a bow and a quiver of around twenty arrows. The two were excellently skilled in combative skills that could destroy an onslaught of beings upon will. Samhain had wondered their use to him in the ranging of battles to come against the spoken adversaries of destruction.

At this point Samhain's intuition is in question and his direction of action is as cloudy as the gloomy sky upon a rain storm. His depiction of the storm challenges his understanding of a reign of horrible terror. A terror that is to bound him to his knees, to the death as a priest. There has to be a way to overcome the fall of his sanctuary, but how is what he asked himself being unsure of how to accept the task. What is the will of these priests that they felt the need to contact him in a challenging manner as their first solution? Will they burrow in with me to make an end to this escapade that's taking corruption into my sanctuary?

"Brother believe us, we understand the feelings that you are being overwhelmed with, this new discovery and know that we are here to help in the discomforts of understanding the issue."

The priests' suggestion held some light that had moved Samhain to a more gratifying feeling of ease.

"That is something to be said to ease my void of understanding. How will you be of help in the future is a desirable question that I now ask."

Aiding Samhain and to answer his question the talkative priest grabs the orb and began rubbing the sphere. The orb begins to illuminate, creating more light than what was already within the room. A pictorial had surfaced and the two priests have taken part in gathering the scholars and the priest of other cities to a united army. The picture had amazed Samhain with major relief that his work has not been undone.

"That is not all of it," the priest interjected.

The orb filters a picture of a wolf standing face to face with Samhain and that the two prepare for a face off. Samhain is shocked to see this ideally that it was the same picture that the two priest have come to warn him about.

"This will become a chapter for you great priest. At the time of your facing you alone will have to deliver the blow that will seal your own faith. As times like this have come before us it will be up to you to manage how you will live, as to how you will survive."

The priest was right, and it will be up to Samhain and how he finishes this war of man, beast and the undead.

~ ~ ~

The night drew long until the up rise of the sun as it flared its firm rays upon Central. The night had overtaken the scholars at the sanctuary as they slept long from a weary night. Moans encased the sanctuary that led straight to Maxins' room. Within range of the morning heat, the early light has started its array of dawn. The wounded priest gasps for air in his duration of pain that has bestowed his body. He yelps loudly in sheer pain that nobody could manage to turn away from him. All scholars young and old could not turn away from the loud cry. The students turned in their beds trying to catch a moment more of rest yet it wouldn't allow them any further.

"Somebody please make it stop," a younger scholar cries out while lying in his bed.

"Aaah!," Maxin cries.

"That's it," the student demands. "Sometimes you have to do things yourself."

The boy argued the means of the yelling to himself and decides to check on it by himself. He hopped out of his bed like a frog searching for water and scattered to the door. As he opens it Maxin yells once more, "IT BURNS FOR THE LIFE OF ME, PLEASE HELP."

The boy was frightened by the cry this time around and thought to himself that he maybe needed a hand. After thinking of gathering help the boy rushed to the sides of Buckner and Cash.

Out of all the scholars these two had proven to the boy that they could be more helpful than Brett or any other scholar.

"Help! Help." The boy yelled while shaking the two scholars. "Maxin needs help."

Buckner sits up in his bed as Cash had followed before hearing another cry from Maxin.

"Ahhh…"

"Come on," the boy harps.

With everything of a full concern for the boy the two jump to the boy's aide as they rush to Maxins' side. Footsteps filled the narrow hall as they ran down its limited space. '*Squeak*', the door creaked upon being rammed open by the three scholars. Smoke filled the air at the sight that Maxin was being burned alive.

~ ~ ~

"So far these days are still in our corner, and there are many more to come after." Jasper incited.

The political figure foiled a glass of red wine under his nose as he pulls a long hard drag of its scent. Too many people of elegant thinking they would surely believe that they have come in contact with a saint. Being the don to his followers as he is praised at the beckoning of his great mentoring to others and how he manages to see a greater light in things. The man's rise to glory doesn't cause him to feel guilty to being an heir of a passing lineage of politicians. No, the glory is out done to how cunning he is in measuring the scope of others mindscape and to how well he fulfills them.

"Time is our better half," Jasper proclaimed. " If I wasn't so wholehearted in retrieving the love and joys that others have long forgotten then I wouldn't be the figure that I am."

He preaches to his staff of four members that lay waiting for all of his demands to come. They sat silently in his quarter with no regard in giving ideas or any demands of their own. Thus they love the politician as if he was the sole caretaker of theirs that they couldn't turn away from. By his people alone he is what he has become, a true contort of power.

"Is anyone listening or am I alone on this one. I mean it!" Jasper exclaims.

All four staff members began speaking at once to give the politician praise, a team of stooges who resist for anything above the great politician Jasper. Not much of what he deserves, he's encouraged because it's what he wants.

"Alright now," Jasper begins speaking. "I'm starting to think that I can't be anymore appreciated then what I am. But why, why am I beginning to think that I'm losing the concerns of my dear followers."

None of his staff members spoke at all. The last out spoken staff member was used as meat to feed the dogs. Being a politician is one thing, but being the head of vampires draws a significant line that shouldn't dare be erased. The politician proves to be the ambiguous type and his staff team is very well aware of it.

"Oh well I'm bored, now someone please tell me where that one eyed dreadful witch has gone to!"

The head of staff team points to two of his members, directing them to Jaspers subject. A few minutes later the two return with the witch of one eye that he speaks of.

"The great politician calls on me, what troubles you sir?" She asked.

"Yes, sister I am troubled." He says in a studious tone. "I feel like my followers are beginning to lose faith in me. I want to touch their hearts once again to draw them a bit closer to me. But how is the thing that discourages me, out of what fashion can this be done? Please tell me while I'm all ears!"

Jasper props his hands under his chin to hold his head as he leaned onto his desk. He was very impotent and he let it be known by his drawing of interest in the witch. She gave a smile before coming to terms of speaking. The witch wanted to be sure that Jasper understood that she couldn't see the future without her eye. Cheerfully she held her palm out face up as she cringe her fingers, crimping for her return.

"Oh fine, it doesn't do me any good anyway." Jasper states as he hands her an orb.

"Precious so precious eye. It's good to see you once again. Awe what do you have for me today, what is it that the politician thinking of?" The witch confined to her eye as she rubs it.

The orb glows white inside of the dim room and a picture appears. It was clear for the witch to see but it wasn't enough to get a full idea just yet.

"This picture shows so much less, if you may give me a second or third eye then maybe I can finish the depiction at a greater understanding." The witch stated.

"You do know I can't say no to that." Jasper responds.

He then pulled two more orbs from the desk and handed them to the witch. She marveled at his ability to provide that which she asked for.

"Any more and you would have decapitated all of my sisters." The witch stated.

Jasper didn't say much on top of the chuckle that he had let out. It was very humorous to him because he knows that he would destroy them all if he ever had to. To someone like himself who knows about the limits to live and the mysterious unknown it's a given understanding about the orbs.

"The less of what I have, yet it should do you well for what I ask of you." Jasper stated.

"And it is," the witch replied.

The picture becomes animated and it displays more than what Jasper expects, a party.

~~~
~~~

"I want to see more!" Samhain explains. The two priest gave each other an eerie look and assumed Samhain was awake. They knew he knows that it takes more than one orb to further create a sighting yet did he know that they were missing the other two.

"Brothers from the far city, tell me more of this found story." He asked.

"Sorry brother," the priest starts. "This is not our time to do so you see, when just a couple of days past we saw this of you out of this one orb."

"But you carry the most orbs available, handed to you at your large monastery. Wait, something happened and you beckon me from the fault." Samhain replies.

"We haven't worked with this as a purpose of our own. You would have mistaken us with that thought to hold onto. No brother, we too are looking for help with this one orb of our original four. We are clueless to how this has happened yet it discourages us that a few of our scholars were injured during that fight.

For them we searched for this level of peace that we might be able to find with you sir." The second priest stated.

"So far I'm starting to understand what I couldn't as I believe we're right in the middle of something big. Something so big that intends to consume us in the midst of its reign." Samhain stated. "I don't know how it's all tying up but I do know a pack of wolves are wondering around out there somewhere in a cave in the Black Forest. That was when I lost one of my own orbs."

Samhain pulls out the lasting orb from his satchel and places it onto the table." Take another look with the second eye."

The white priest did just as Samhain asked of him as he rubbed both orbs. It was then when he noticed the cave again, his lost orb, and something about that kid that he tried to hypnotize. All of it coming to some type of balance that he's even more clueless about. What does it all mean, if it could come to him any faster?

"Samhain assured the two priests that he could manage to keep to whatever plan that they can come up with. It was at that point that it became clear to Samhain that roughly things will have to take place by ear. The priest told Samhain that they will return home to the far city and begin preparations for what is to come. Before doing so the talkative priest handed Samhain his orb back.

"We're coming back to reunite with you." The white priest insisted.

The men shared their concerns for one another as they parted ways. Samhains plate of steak and eggs were still warm to the touch as he begun to finish his meal. The two priest had exit the bar when the second priest was bumped by the same guy that had ran into Samhain just hours earlier.

"I'm sorry, so sorry," the guy blurts as he darts right past them.

The blood on his collar had nearly run wild as he headed for the bar. The man was frantic in his actions, fear had consumed him.

"Ambrose," he yelled.

He was looking for his new wife in marriage of the last two weeks. Outside of the beast that startled him, he couldn't stand to be away from the one that he loved. His heart poured for her as he continued searching for her, "Ambrose."

The cries tore loudly in the small space and then she appeared. Her golden hair draped over her blue eyes that she pulls back with two of her fingers.

"Genesis!" she yells back.

She appeared from behind him, rubbing his shoulder as he stared away, started at first he jumped before noticing her. The two had embraced from a moment of disarray. Ambrose was confused, she just saw him a few hours earlier that day. Was he that madly in love, with her that he just had to see her? No, it was something far more of a void of understanding.

Genesis was trembling badly and the wound on his collar was worsening. From that she knew it couldn't be by any other reasoning that this happened.

"Oh my gosh, your bleeding! What happened?" she asks him.

She takes him by his hand before he can speak, leading him to the same room as where Samhain sat in peace. The loud thud of the door opening startles the priest.

"Oh sorry," Ambrose says. "Thought it was empty in here."

"It is fine, I was just finishing up." Samhain replies giving a long gaze at Genesis.

"Who is he?" Genesis wonders. "I've seen him before earlier today.

"Please allow me to introduce myself I'm Samhain, priest of Central. We met at a garden down the road."

"Yes, at my garden. I remember now." Genesis replies. "Your injured please sit. I have medicine for that." Samhain implies.

He reaches into his satchel bypassing the orb, at the moment the boy is not a real threat yet Samhain doesn't want that to change. Genesis sits while Ambrose leaves to get a wet warm cloth. Samhain stirs the conversation a little bit.

"What happened to ya kid?" he asks.

"I don't know exactly, you wouldn't believe me if I had told you anyway so don't bother to act like you care." Genesis replied.

He felt hopeless, how anyone would believe if he told them that a wolf had attacked him. Nobody believes in such a fairy tale and why would a priest be any different. He remained silent about the ordeal and allowed the priest to clean his wound.

"It must have been something pretty fierce to cause this gash on you kiddo, you sure don't want to talk about it?" Samhain pleaded to the younger man.

For what it was worth to Genesis' the silence was golden.

The silence had irritated the priest to a point of almost no return. Why was the young man targeted and why had he tried to reach him himself? Was it some silly coincidence or not? Either way they are playing the game on the same field. Samhain opens up a bit, warming Genesis to his questioning.

"This gash looks as if a giant beast could have done this, and it's not an average cut, that I can tell."

Genesis was reluctant to give an immediate response, yet he did want to lean into the ideal that Samhain had suggested. Before long Ambrose reappeared with a warm cloth and iodine. The generic first aid that she had wasn't a match to Samhain's special batch. She then finished cleaning from where the wound had touched his lower shoulder.

"You should try to be safe at times. You will forever be a target if you don't secure yourself against any real dangers." Samhain stated.

"That's wise, but whatever the creature had thought I was going to be its food for a minute there. I mean I ran into a barn and it ate two chickens." Genesis claims.

"I can tell." Ambrose states while pulling on the blood splatter on the left side of his face. "This can't be your blood."

"Right, the chickens weren't so lucky." Genesis stated.

Samhain got quiet as he zoned out the conversation that was taking place, remarkably in deed. What kind of creature would leave from a foot chase then tear into a cage of hens. Only one comes to mind as he understands that he had been followed. If that's the case then he could be next among the others. This town needs to be fled and soon.

~~~

Nattuck enters the room to the squeals of his brother. Like everyone else, he's squeamish to see the blistered skin of Maxin bubbling and oozing.

"Great God," Nattuck screams. "Get him out of here."

The four males all grabbed onto Maxin's mat with two of them on each side. Together they moved him into the hallway far from the blistering sun. He began to smell of melted flesh that bubbled altogether. The young scholar began to throw up at the look and stench of the raw flesh.

"Please you two, can you cover the windows." Nattuck demands.

The upper portion of the window was cased in by bars, so the scholars took bed sheets and tied them off. The sunlight was still fairly shining through yet the bulk of it was cutoff. They did this again toward the two remaining windows. The room had dimmed down with very little light shining in, as Maxin began to rest again.

"Elee, Elee," Nattack yells for her aide.

His voice echoes yet she wasn't around to answer, possibly
~~~

she was taking the time to bathe. Early morning baths were continuously idea of hers, that she would have a grade of peace to herself.

The young scholar had caught wind of his stomach as he stopped. All eyes were on him as the scholars had peered into the hallway.

"What's going on?" Sicily asks.

"Nothing for the rest of you to be bothered with," Nattuck stated, yet nobody listened.

The hallway was soon swarmed with scholars, as they all were curious as to what happened to Maxin. The awes of the scholars echo the hallway as they stood in Maxin's room. The sight was terrifying to them. The scene was questionable to everyone except for the priest Nattuck. It hits him hard as he was left unbalanced with overpowering thoughts of what to do. Was he chosen to fulfill a test of reason? A surreal deity to something that was beyond his control!

Nattuck knows to think higher of the situation and not doubt the truth of what was going on; a war is at hand. The priesthood had just become a part in it and there was more to come. Nattuck dismissed the scholars and selected Cash and Sicily for rations detail for the morning. A few students whooped in cheering to see Sicily making the meals again. To them she services the best tasting everything.

All the scholars were preparing for morning lessons while

Cash and Sicily spoke about a relative conversation. To them the sight was uncanny and things weren't adding up. Why was Alana hidden in the basement and now Maxin is harmed by sunlight. This was not making much sense to the scholars, especially to the issue about Maxin. Where in the world do they find these types of things, and did they both coincide.

The thought that has hammered in Sicily mind more than Cash is to be questioning what is happening. How much are they really missing of the important information? Do as we're told and not as we may feel, isn't how this works! Well Sicily knew that they needed some answers and maybe Alana could answer a few. After they prepared breakfast; oatmeal and grilled cheese, Sicily figured they could take a minute to gather a few answers.

Cash was very hesitant at first but it took some convincing. It's not every day that people harbor a friendly ghost that can speak.

"The truth shall set us free," Sicily joked.

It wasn't easy getting away from the others and without Buckner they felt a bit odd, but the day had to go on. The chow hall was cramped and Nattuck was stuck watching over the others so they still did well. Only a few minutes in the basement nearly felt like an eternity. Sicily called for Alana in a hushed whisper and couldn't get an answer. Before they had thought it was no use and time to leave Cash had notice something moving around. To his luck he called Alana's name yet only to his surprise it was Elee.

"What are you doing down here?" She asked them.

The two were stumped and couldn't initially give in to the truth. Cash tried to cover by saying he believes a scholar had wondered down there while no one was watching. For the worth of it Elee couldn't deny him that much of a concern as she escorted the two back upstairs.

"Almost, and we're so close!" Sicily whispered to herself.

Best part was they weren't sure they were in the right place, and now they were in order with everyone else. They didn't see where she went after she spoke to Nattuck, they just expected to hear about it later on.

"Where have you been, everyone is talking about Maxin, and I mean everybody!" Buckner stated pressing in between the two.

"Something's not right!" Sicily says.

"I agree, Elee didn't even want to punish us for wandering away." Cash mentioned. "Ever since they came back from their journey… it hasn't been the same."

"Cash is right," Sicily insists, "what are we really getting prepared for?"

"Maybe it's the end of the world!" Buckner exclaimed.

~ ~ ~

It was probably the last night that Samhain would be staying in Idel. He knew he had to make a move and it had to be soon.

What was he going to do to connect with the people of Idel? His hopes were lost and for some reason the kid Genesis is going to make a mark to tie up an end to this new powerhouse, at least he believed so. He believed to keep intact with the finances of the new sanctuary and that was of Genesis.

That was it, why control what he can't instead of what he can. The guy Genesis has to be the answer and Samhain could tell. The priest finally finished eating his meal before retracting to return his plate to the bar when he noticed that Genesis was still there. He tried hard to keep his will and intentions unnoticed as he kept eye of the young man. He knew he had to get into the man's mind and direct him to Central.

Before Genesis leaves the bar, Samhain made his presence be known. He walked to the man to shake his hand. As he did his eyes fluttered a white glow and Samhain had made it very clear that he was to see the man in Central. Genesis nodded and gives him an assurance that only at the right time will he do so. That was the last time Samhain would see Genesis in person. Preparations were made for Samhain to obtain a horse and some bread that he was on his way to leaving Idel with his hope set forth for Central.

The two men parted ways and Genesis was set to go back home as his wife worked the bar. The night wind was cold and the moon was out. Owls howled and hooted at the dark night and the roads were empty. He didn't walked far before the night began to siege a dark cold chill at heart. A lining of woods stood before Genesis home and a treacherous being waited for his approach.

Just before entering into his home the lurking beast approaches once again. It snarled and ravished its teeth preparing to stare into Genesis to finish the kill. The man was terrified at the account and tried to enter into the home. At the closing of his door the beast had burst in before he could lock the door. Genesis was now trapped within his own home.

Whatever that wasn't stuck to the ground, Genesis threw at the snarling beast to fight free from its prowl. It wasn't enough to keep the beast away until a lit lantern was knocked over. The candle fell out and rolled on top of the wool rug that was underneath the wolf. Instantly the home was a blaze and then the wolf was gone. Genesis laid on the ground watching his home go up in flames in amazement; he knew that this could have only been an act of God.

There was no possible way to figure out how much fire had consumed the home. It was a loss at the most and fear had once again come over Genesis. It wasn't long before he remembered seeing Samhain telling him that he had a second home, a place that sought for his attention, this place was Central. What was becoming of Genesis is a unique oncoming for what was prophesied to happen in time.

~~~

The priest of the far city had alerted Ilam and myself to take watch over Central and become their eyes and ears. Our goal was a simple task of being able to catch any and all angles of suspicious activities that outlasted an average day.
~~~

Clues, clues, and more clues is what we searched for in real hopes of being able to understand the awful preceding. Nothing is what we came up with except for the Politicians campaign drawing large speculations with his night ball, the Night of the Politician. The day we found out about the werewolves we were already a day way too late. Torn clothes were found scattered throughout the silent streets of Central as my husband Ilam assured me to keep moving onward. That was when Jasper had taken full control of Central's militia and campaigned for the bordering cities to do the same.

Jasper was then praised in its irony as the people had begun to call him a protector of life. They did this as a substantial gift from the people of Central who all had known his people well. Not much can be said about Central that wouldn't bring fire to a desirable fight to the priesthood. Above all, is the fact that it's already determined that change will definitely come. Allow me to retract that last statement, change is a forum compared to the events that took place.

The priest of the far city had seen me fit to be added to the priesthood that Samhain had protocol. By the time we arrived we had much to talk about. We discussed the missing orbs from the far city and how they believed vampires were conspiring to make an unsuspecting revolt to power. A discussion that I had seen to be way too unreal as the times had unraveled. But this was a time of mystery and by great design it was a time of understanding.

"I would never have thought it so, Sasha," Samhain

remarked. "To see this time in our lives as being the darkest times anyone had ever seen in history."

It was as if it was a bad dream folding together to a defiant ending. He immediately gave me rank among his priesthood and told the others to give into any initial recording of me. Fair to say it was worth the commenting as I had enacted within the priesthood as a priestess. My husband Ilam took his guard with the church that was attached to the sanctuary.

I didn't realized that on Sundays they would all attend service as we had done my first Sunday. It was a special day that I joined more to the coming of a couple from Idel. Genesis and Ambrose of course at the side of their brother Clad. Upon Pastor Johns' offer for meet and greet my Ilam and I had thought we should become close to them. Not only had Samhain had guaranteed them closure, yet they bloomed of love. A naturalist trait thus would prove valuable in times of fears and pain.

One might consider asking how I could tell and it surely goes into certain actions. The boy looked strong and agile but bore a timid rigidness. That was probably due to his endearing commitment to Ambrose that had enacted his change in stability. The girl was proud yet she carried a shield of peace and happiness, and I can tell it was because of Genesis. They came because Genesis stated that Samhain would make a home for them in a time of need.

He swore to the extent of his life that Idel had become wroth with vermin that was making it to unbearable to live there. He said he pictured the life with his wife to be one that was more favorable than death or carnage. Yet to himself he prayed that he wouldn't have to face the large fanged beast ever again and vowed to his wife that he would protect her until death.

The two had agreed prior on that life is what had brought them to the priesthood. Nothing more than a piercing glance at its best could tell about these two. There was more than just that which made this day so important and it was the announcements. The announcement, that we had heard, was about the 'Night of the Politician' that's scheduled to be held here in Central. It was a more beckoning kind of a day for me yet more was to come.

"And here you go," I said showing the guest to their room.

The chapel had its own basement to relation of the sanctuary. Within the basement there were many rooms that were locked and off limits to the average visitor of the church. Still in the same the facility was large enough to occupy more than enough people than imaginable. Clad was offered a room of his own as Ambrose and Genesis stayed closer to each other in this time of need. They were curious yet at peace.

"Has priest Samhain given any inkling as to what we are required to do for our stay?" Genesis asked me.

I had assured him that it was at the least Samhain's sanctuary yet they stayed in tied of the chapel and away from the priesthood, at least for now. "Pastor John is the one who will consider options for your stay."

It wouldn't be too long before the pastor would be putting them to work in the chapel. It was a great move for the pastor and the priesthood at the most. But it was still a question of how in the world does this group tie in to the sanctuary and how would Samhain yet get them to entwine. The odds were still in the hands of Samhain when I left my statement with the group as I returned to my own room. I was sleeping in Maxins' old quarters where my husband and I had made the place a bit more comfortable to stay.

Maxin on the other hand, well he grew to different distinctiveness. It was only the day after his brutal awakening that he had fully healed. It wasn't anything that was natural about it and it shook me and my husband for a moment. We wondered how and we really couldn't question the odds to the reality about it. This was when I had learned about the truth of the discipline that the priesthood had driven so roughly to its takers.

Samhain accepted him still as a relic to the priesthood. I couldn't understand it but Samhain came to tie me to the realization that we were dealing with something far outside of our realm of power and we needed new strengths. He began relying on the idea that Maxin had turned into a vampire and in a sorrowful pain he became lonely. The priest was lonely enough that he made Elee his next of power.

"This is nothing that we should run from; instead it is something that needs to be embraced." Samhain stated.

"But why, how, can this even be possible? I have never dreamt of understanding a vampire and never have I believed that

I would come this close to one in my life." Sasha states.

"What is it Samhain that has beckoned us to become beings of unnatural proportions." Elee commits.

"Yes proportions that is very different than the ones who had done this to you. In their heart is greed, or possibly hatred for the mankind. Yet you lived to be the pedestal that breaks that curse of a feel." Samhain claims.

"I'm charmed by your words, like always Samhain, yet what do you mean by this? What is it that you have in mind?" Elee stated.

"Glad you asked, it's all about history and the truthfulness within the stories that have been told. History says that if the head of the vampires is killed then the unborn vampire may, just may be able to retain their normal life." Samhain claimed.

"This is madness, how can that be true that vampires have roamed for thousands of years." Maxin states.

"That is something that can be said yet is undermined, let's be serious we never really thought that the stories of vampires were real but it's the faith in the concept that keeps the mind boggled." Samhain replied.

"For years I laughed at the many dis-beliefs of this world and that was until I met you, now I have to agree that my body is different and maybe history does has its own way of making reality." Maxin expressed.

"I want this to be real so I'm not taking no for any answers. What are we about to do next?" Elee inquired.

~ ~ ~

"She is beautiful, as beautiful as the midnight stars, she's as beautiful as the days early sunrise, as beautiful as me even."

"Are we going to keep her boss."

"This is something I would have to come to grips with since we have lost our way with the vampires. They love to deceive us, and think we don't know what they may truly be about."

"Our demise."

"A demise that will falter at their own descent, two hands may idle in different ways from one another and still don't know how the other one is in accord."

"Good one Lucky, but how is that the same as us, what will we do?"

"The far city is within our reach and Idel is taking numbers by the day, let's make a stand that will capture the world by surprise!"

"ALL HAIL LORD LUCKY!"

~ ~ ~

The blood shed within the streets have been overlooked by the politician and his call for a party wasn't really driving the priesthood. I knew better than to be engulfed by this idea and I knew that we have to face what was at hand. It was odd to find the wolf in Idel, yet still a very possible option to encounter it again. I wanted to create an extraction team to head back to the far city and warn our brothers there. With the fact that Samhain gave his word to me that I may take three of his best scholars at the bonding hands that Maxin and Elee both agree to accompany.

A six man team is very ideal to be the victors in this war that lay hand to the priesthood. For what it is worth the construction of unifying is the key, strength by numbers.

~~~

"Hush before we all get caught. Who knows how long we have before they all come back." Sicily said.

"I still think something big is about to happen and we might be right smack in the middle of it." Cash implied.

"Yet she still might be able to help…" Buckner stated.

"Help with what?" Alana asks.

"We need you to tell us what you may know about your death. Plus why did they try to banish you here?" Sicily asks.

"Oh, this is very sudden. I really haven't put much thought to what you asked me before." Alana said.

"Please, something weird is going on and we need answers. You said you knew Samhain, sometime before you died." Cash asked.
~~~

"Yes" Alana responded.

"Then you may know something else, something that could have led him to creating the priesthood." Buckner states.

"Is that what you want to know? If I knew why he started the priesthood?" Alana asks.

"No" Sicily cried out. "We want to know more than just that. Like why were you killed?"

"Even then I really didn't know it could have been for money!" Alana stated.

"Money!" Sicily commented. "If they killed you then they couldn't have gotten any money."

"Actually they still could have," Buckner replied, "a ransom."

"But who would do such a thing. Maybe it was somebody who had no end to what they could manage in life. It could have been somebody that was torn from the reality of everybody else and an isle of their own." Cash states.

"It's more than that!"

"Who are you?" Sicily asked.

"I am Andrea and it was way more than you are to believe and more than I actually understand."

"What do you mean?" Sicily asks.

"I mean my family, led by my husband Morgan, was very skilled in acquiring money, maybe a little too well! Though with all thought I don't believe they would never give in to defeat to any fight. We we're skilled in armed combat from traditional means, which that tradition ended with the death of us." Andrea states.

"Somebody feared you?" Sicily asked.

"Possibly!" a voice answered. "We grew to be well proportioned in many things.

"Like what?" Hunting, carving, fishing, gardening, building, and politics," the voice said.

"Uncle Joe," Alana cried.

"But still we feared no man." A voice said.

"Cash, Buckner." Sasha called out.

"Please, whoever did this to us will pay, and we need your help. Hopefully we can figure this out together." Joe said.

"If this is true then, how is it that we can help you? Aren't you stuck here?" Sicily asked.

"No. Without the banish spells the containment of us is to our own freedom. But we can possess. Let us possess you all and find out this horrid mystery together." Joe asked.

"Sicily!" Sasha yelled.

The three emerged from the stairwell without being seen. It

wasn't too long after that they had bumped into Sasha.

"Oh there you are, where have you been?" Sasha asked.

"Training." Sicily responds.

"Well, from how I hear it you three are the best in the sanctuary and I have a mission for us." Sasha implied.

"A mission." The three commented in unison.

"Yes, together we are going to head for the far city and stay at the sanctuary there. How does that sound for an adventure?" Sasha stated.

The group couldn't come up with any form of denial even if they hadn't ever thought about leaving the sanctuary. To them it was a song of music being played and they hadn't known the title of the song. What will they do? How will they survive in thc far city? What was it for them to do?

"Sounds nice," Buckner replied.

"Nice in deed, so nice in fact, just for our safety we will be trailed by Maxin and Elee and they will keep a close eye upon us. Now how does that sound to you?" Sasha asked.

"Sounds like we better get some rest. When are we leaving?" Cash asked.

"In two days we will begin this journey, but from how I see it Samhain agrees that he would accept this as your chance to journey to priesthood and return into the sanctuary as either a priest or a priestess for the lady. Well now how about that?" Sasha inquired.

Wow, finally the pit of conception is finally upon them and they don't have any words to say about it. I wonder how much of a childhood it was that they haven't really lived. So much for worrying that I couldn't, it would shame me way too much to even think of the worst situation possible. Now was supposed to be important and I felt like I could have just gotten these kids killed.

"No. Priestess, we are very excited to hear about this, it's just we don't feel like we're ready." Sicily stated.

"Speak for yourself." Cash replied. "I only need to understand how we will survive."

"Yes of course. More training is called for but we will manage. So tomorrow we will review and go over some tips for travel and then we will settle that score." Sasha explained.

"Great," Buckner said.

What can I say, we are in a position to being place to the test but what a better way for adaptive learning than the real thing. It wasn't my plan at all to turn these kids into a brute force but we had to try to keep up to the disasters. I relieved them for bed.

"Just like that?" Constable Greg asked.

"Yes, it was late and it was already too much for them to handle so I let them go."

Somebody had to check back on Maxin and Elee and I do believe even they weren't ready for what was to come. I walked into the sparring room where they had been practicing with one another before I heard the both of them chatting.

"I still don't get it!" Elee said. "If you haven't brought me into this then I wouldn't have to worry so much about whether or not if you will become a threat."

"If I become a threat! You have officially lost your marbles." Maxin responds.

"I've lost my marbles? I've been marked you selfish dope."

"To talk about selfishness as I stand a marked man myself and yet I still bare the bearings to stay in check and not taking a single advantage of the priesthood and you call me selfish "

"You don't really have a choice." Elee replied.

The both of them were making contact as they continued sparring, it seemed as if this thing could have become out of context. Elee rushed and struck at Maxin with her wooden sword only to have been evaded at every mark. They were getting used to the new skill sets that they had acquired and I can tell. The agility of Maxin was remarkable and I even seen him come to a hovering haul at times. This was my first real sight of the power that the vampires contained.

"But you have to admit, these are some very sweet powers that we now have!" Maxin stated.

Sweet was a taste less than sorry for how Elee had felt about her new adaption. She really could care less. She was now less than human, but more of a disastrous freak of nature. She contested every comment of comfort that Maxin had to offer. To describe it, bitter wouldn't even be considerable of the pain of loss that she had felt.

"I would still rather die, than mark myself of this piteous reality of death. We are dead in the eyes of the world." Elee stated.

She then charged at him in a cork screw spin with her sword drawn. Forcing Maxin to take his next move she then levitated above his body to unleash a heavy body slam of her own. The slam had caused a forceful blow to Maxin that he hit his face upon the floor and blood began to rush from his mouth.

"A wondrous blow to such a dirty mouth!" Elee exclaimed.

Angered, Maxin hissed and snarled with his fangs drawn to attack as he too began an attack of his own. It was to my mystery that I didn't break up the fight, that they may have been able to overpower me. Elee evaded the large man as he rushed with anger. He was distraught in my eye, even manic, for what he had done to that woman. Though he didn't care, he flustered on and on…

"Do you think I chose this…"

He charged at her as he pinned to lay a blow across her chest. Elee lifted from the floor where she began walking upon the ceiling. A smart move but bold beyond her best understanding of these powers. It was then I had to recall that life was limitless and that maybe boldness was a death defying act to ensure what we really needed. I watched onward to only see the two move as if they were above all life in a horrid dance of death and pain.

"So you began to have pity upon them." Constable Greg asked.

"It was not pity; I only agreed that in the need of choices that is when you will truly began to feel alive."

"So what did you do next?" Constable Greg asked.

I stopped them.

"Stop!" I said.

With his angered look, Maxin addressed me. "How long have you been there?"

"Long enough to know that you two are starting to enjoy what you are becoming." I said.

"What we are, at last someone would agree that what we are becoming is something that may be of some good for the priesthood." Maxin replied.

"No, and yet if that is what you believe then, sure." I said.

Maxin brushed the blood from his mouth as Elee kept an eyeful watch of his movements. It wasn't the first yet I'm sure it won't be the last time that she would keep watch of him.

"We need to make plans." I said.

Something strange carried on. It was only as if we had adapted to this unshakable new reality that nobody was ready for. Still within the break of the early sunlight it was questioned what was going on with the vampires and how things have taken place.

~ ~ ~

"Eureka! We have it at last, and for once in my life things are coming to me in full fashion and I love it. We should call the event 'The Night of the Politician' who could have come up with a better idea?" Jasper stated.

"Sir," a voice stirs from the distance.

"Oh," Jasper responds. "Please come in and share my wonderful joy."

"Yes Sir," the man said.

"So what have we come up with now?" Jasper asked.

"Doing as I was told. I've come to realize that the priesthood has come up with an idea of uniting the sanctuary with the far city." The man said.

"This is true you say, well then we will have to make ourselves acquainted then." Jasper replies.

"Sir, we could allow them to rush in, with our eyes around the ground we can manage to…" the man stopped.

"Haven't you had enough ideas for once? I am well aware of

the eyes that are available and I said we will attack the group while they are at travel." Jasper said.

~~~

The way I hear it, we weren't the only ones taking a bashing about what was becoming of ourselves. It was hard for Genesis to come out to admit the terror that he was under when the wolf came. He sheltered his words by covering how it came back to feast on him and tearing through the house. Clad wasn't being all the way honest with everybody, at least not toward his brother. He just sat and watched Ambrose and Genesis talk.

"Can you believe this? We just picked up and left and have a whole new life," Ambrose stated.

"Yeah, I just feel that it was something that had to be done; a something that at least would protect us, for our safety!" Genesis said.

"Something that wasn't that bad of a decision based on the heavy scars that you got. Not to mention our home burning down." Ambrose said.

"Sooner or later it could have been anyone other than me and I don't know how I would be able to handle that. If I ever lost you, Ambrose I would just die." Genesis stated.

He became closer to Ambrose that night, and Clad on the other hand was silent and distant. The next few days were simple and I handled the task of showing the scholars how to make a
~~~

defensive trap for game. We slept easily or at least the scholars did.

"We need to make a goal for our new positions here at the priesthood. We're different now and that is going to stand out to the scholars." Elee stated.

"And so what we are different now, I still hold strongly to my will of grace with a sword and my earnest desire for God. Nothing has changed within me." Maxin petitioned.

"Foolish man, do you think this type of responsibility comes without a challenge of its own? How dare you expect me to want to reason with such an option? Whatever that comes of this can't be too good," Elee stated.

It was all too easy to say that she was right. The two had then begun to fight inside of the sparring room. Both of them drew wooden swords against each other in a battle of will. I watched onward and not planned to intervene and become a victim of the fight but I realized something. The life we live is built less of options of our own but by the summoning of others and the destiny that lies together. The two fought a long fight as if they had danced in the harmony of battle, taking shots at one another and making mores space between the two. I had had enough.

"Stop it now! What will the scholars think of this if they notice the agreeing of vengeance and blood that you two have settled for one another." I said.

"It is the design that was given to us that allows this as an acceptable act and not the worries of children." Maxin stated.

"Am I not older than children that I worry about the sake of them all? You two should have more integrity than that," I said.

The cold silence broke the ravaged sparring room that led way for priestess Elee to comment to me that I was right. They had realized that I haven't forgotten what the priesthood had to deliver for the future of the scholars. It delivered a future of a prize for advancement that has been sought out by so many before them. The night had worn more than an unsettled bond of grief and anguish as I wasted hours of my time trying to put myself together. It was only weeks ago that the inner peace that I carried could take on any bound before I came to Central and lived with the priesthood.

The early dawn had prepared me for the night to come that we will leave for the far city. We had to cross a river in the northeast part of Central and I had already mapped out our course. With Samhain back, he was willing to take back control of the priesthood for the remainder of the time to come yet he still questioned the forgoing of his leaders of the priesthood. Elee on one hand strained a positive control of herself as she spent her time creating a sham to act as curtain for the inside of the carriage. To my eyes she was a step closer to her peak of reasoning and acceptance than Maxin could have ever been.

I spent a few hours watching Samhain giving a lecture for the morning even though he said he would mix things in between combative training. I kept my thoughts mine as I wondered if the scholars were even able to keep up with the strain of the activities that would lay before them. I myself hadn't really known how I would manage yet the thought about it left me speechless. After eating lunch I sent the team of scholars to rest to be prepared to be up for a few hours of our night travel. At sunset we took off with a set of spare clothes and a few items for cooking.

"So you're now telling me that you prepared to leave with a pair of blood thirsty vampires to my city, and that is when we found the four of you! Then what have happened to the two vampires?" Constable Greg ask.

"I don't know!" Sasha responds.

"Sir there has been a break in inside of the front office and I think you should come take a look," the Constable said.

"You stay here, I'll be back shortly." Constable Greg said.

I don't know what they are up to but I can bet that it wasn't anything that would give a significantly good outcome for the Constables. I need to get my head straight, but I don't believe that it would be anytime soon. I tried to think but the banging and loud noise within the background wouldn't let me keep my peace. I think I heard a loud scream coming from the front office when Maxin had appeared.

"I think it's time to leave now," Maxin said.

And that we did as we rushed toward the priesthood of the far city to see if anything had become of it. The city's streets were empty like a cold chilled night that had sent everyone indoors. It wasn't too surprising as it was just minutes to midnight and the hours stretching up further. The priesthood wasn't too far from the police station as we ran a few blocks further East. We couldn't bear to rethink about what had taken place there.

It was as if it was all a dream and we were the main characters that survived the final thrashing. Blood shed that tore the entrance of the sanctuary with trails and splatter from top to bottom. I knew that this was a possibility but it was a sight to actually see. I didn't remember the details as to being this horrific or even as daunting as this had become. Something tells me that this isn't the end and at some point a change would incur a major difference in this fight.

If only we had made it out of the carriage in time then none of this would even be possible. I was chosen by the priesthood to see this through and it's becoming way too terrifying to believe. The chosen one and it's my entire fault. I wasted no time in searching for anyone; I knew what we were there to retrieve at this time, the last orb that was being protected by the priesthood.

It laid within the courtyard where a great fight between the wolves and the priesthood had taken place. If I hadn't known any better I could tell by the number of naked individuals scattered all around the premises who was winning this ugly battle. There it was, the orb wrapped tightly around the clutches of one of the dead priests hands, I took it. Maybe this was the chance for me to discover my own path as I soon started recalling the meeting with Jasper at the "Night of the Politician". I stood ready to destroy his whole livelihood as Ilam waited for me.

I was destined to end one leg of this new fight, but why, nobody has ever seen the politician take part in any act yet he held all the cards in hand and all their worth. My hair was ruffled under the midnight breeze as I actively gave account of the orbs records. It would seem that it was all too hard for the others to believe me when I told them that I see us in this place and I ended up with the politician to take him unawares.

"If this is all true Sasha then why would you drag us here? Why haven't you tried to stop any of the recorded acts that were to take place?" Elee asked.

"I don't fully get it either but I can sure bet that when I kill the vulturous Jasper it would then be a victorious day," Sasha said.

"I don't get it," Cash replied. "If that was the case then why act like you were really trying to help us anyway, why add us, why fight at all? Something doesn't sound right."

"Maybe she doesn't believe in herself," Sicily said.

"Maybe I know all too well." Sasha replied. "After all you don't believe that I actually listened to you guys. This isn't just for me, remember. This is also a journey for the six of you."

"Sasha, Elee and I journeyed plenty before and there is only five of us, so what do you mean by the six?" Maxin said.

"The three know what I'm talking about. It is a new time for us all Maxin." Sasha replied.

"What in the world are you talking about?" Elee asked.

Sasha wasn't quick to respond, instead she only handed the orb to Buckner. She gave him a long look and then winked her eye at him. She hoped that he would understand the premise of what she was coming from, she was hoping that eventually he would see it all for himself. "I hope this helps you in understanding what I must do." Sasha said before taking off.

"What? Should we follow her?" Cash asked.

"No" Maxin stated. "As we all assumed something different, we can assure that she won't likely see things taken so lightly."

"Finally we can agree on something." Elee stated. "Though I don't want to get caught anywhere near here when that sun rises, we must look for shelter for the morning to come. You three would have to hold up somewhere safe. Lucky for us you'll be protected for the sunrise are the enemies' true weakness."

"We'll be fine, don't worry about us." Sicily stated.

"We will take refuge among the woods and we would head further south from here. It would be a perfect plan for us to hide out in the city of Idel were Samhain had stayed,." Cash said.

"Good, then we too should find somewhere in the far city to take shelter for the morning." Priest Maxin said.

"But wait, when we get there what are we to do?" Buckner asked.

"Nothing, just get ready for travel and we'll handle the rest." Priestess Elee said.

"We'll be safe, and we will be waiting for you both." Buckner said.

"Same here," the Priestess and Priest said together.

The group of scholars left not knowing what was to be ahead of them yet they knew that the challenge would be a great ordeal. The priestess Elee and priest Maxin on the other hand were tangled in a different type of web. It was up to them to come to find a new carriage with a sense of urgency and fleeing the far city before the come of sunrise. This would be a challenge that wasn't to be held as too difficult to the defiant pair.

~~~

The challenges of the sanctuary were seen as little compared to the depth of what has become of its top scholars. At this time Samhain fancied himself in dealing with the remaining scholars but he wasn't aware, he seemed distracted. From the time that he began his lectures all the way to resting time, he wasn't the most functional as he usually was and hadn't even completed a full task. Time, time and time again was all that rattled his envious soul and broken in the need of progress that he spent his time building. He grumbled to himself about the depiction that he could not cast a full vision.

Though luck alone had saluted many things it had wished to appear to Samhain in a strain of fright. Alone he was in the sanctuary given late night prayers of peace and strength in the stepping of his blindness. It was then when a knock had come to
~~~

the main entrance of temple and that only he alone could answer its call. With only a lantern in his right hand and his prayer beads swaying from the other he walked in faith. The loud thuds shattered through the open hall, *thump, thump, thump.*

He opened the large frame door that would leave him utterly open to any given attack, given no choice by the appearance of his visitor. Nothing could compare to the sense of stale fear that draped within him as he says, "Hello, who goes there?"

"Yes it is I, Jasper." The voice responded.

"It is so late why have you come to brace me with your presence?" Samhain asked with the door wide open.

The man wasn't afraid, nor did he show any form of malicious intent against the priest at last a prayer of peace had been answered.

"I have come to give a formal address if it may be so suitable to you; I only wish to hope to see you at my ball at my estate in this coming of days. I too know how important it is in giving the praise of God his due. I wish to see you aboard our night of events to come." Jasper stated.

"Oh, is that right?" Samhain responded.

"Yes, yes. Would you be so kind enough to invite me in for a brief moment longer? The cold winds are nestling down my back and giving me chills." Jasper stated.

Samhain wasn't too fond of Jasper yet the fact that he was

covered by God did he only allow him in so close to taking his life. The life that God is said to love and those that hated and dwelleth and even creepeth are dangerous to that life.

"Well do so for only a moment." Samhain said.

The politician stepped into the temple alone, for the first time he was away from any followers. It was a sight to see for Samhain that he had the chance of meeting with the politician before at a point in time months, and years earlier. Samhain was so far against stepping into a political position that he frayed away and kept from the temptation that the politician delivered. Tonight was an acceptance to the belief that the priest had a change of heart and will as the unarmed man enter into the priest's facility. The conversation led far from where the priest may had thought yet it draped into a despair of respect for the politician.

"So I haven't seen you much around the political campaign, I almost figured that you could have something against me." Jasper stated.

Samhain hadn't want to get into a detailed argument upon why he hasn't been seen on the political platforms but he still figured that the politician was out of place. It is with the great disdain for this man that the priest fiddled his rosemary beads within his hands, as he decides to curve Jasper's thoughts.

"I am a figure of God and not of the people that wishes not to discern itself with him. That is what makes the two of us very different from one another. We are of different shades in this walk of life and that is why you would not see me on any political platform, even though you seem to want to reach out even more than I would seem to understand at the moment." Samhain said.

"This would be quite true, I do wish to extend myself further to the people and that is why I am expanding the states militia and asking others to join if they may wish. For one I do understand that God does have his place in the war of life. Perhaps I could expand my resources to the one who stands at his right hand, perhaps." Jasper stated.

"Again that would be too close of a discomfort for me as I am here to expand the development of my scholars and to the ones who wish to be seen once a week by God as we celebrate within the church," Samhain said.

Samhain lifted his rosemary bead with the cross in his hand and tried to hand it to Jasper. Reluctantly he declined to even give a quick look at the cross that he bared, for Jasper it held a more challenging power to wield.

"I see, that it would be even harder for you to consider one thing when you have your hands full already, but at what time would you be able to stop the lectures with the scholars and then soon be free of such responsibilities. That is when I would be free to offer a hand to our states militia in giving them a piece of God's hands. Well as I wished to speak I have and now it would be time for me to go, until we meet again, Priest Samhain." Jasper said before leaving.

Samhain was short of any thoughts on what had taken place, yet he knows well that the gesture couldn't have come short of any logical reasoning. The only thing was that Samhain couldn't place his hands on the conclusion of what was going on. While holding the rosemary beads in his hand he fiddled with it more as he plundered his thoughts. Perhaps a chance has awakened itself for the priest to take action of his own.

~ ~ ~

Time was flying by and hours laid midway of the next sunrise and the scholars were tired of walking and searching for a place to rest. It was a moment of reaching for the comfort that they had within the sanctuary that they had dreamed of.

"We may need to stop to rest, without the carriage we would have to set up somewhere outside and start a campfire." Sicily suggested.

"But we are so close to Idel, I can feel it." Cash replied.

"Close isn't the perspective that we should say that we are, we haven't even reached the bridge that connects the two places." Buckner said. "Even then I remember priest Samhain telling Sasha that he made a Troll to mark that one. This Troll would be our sign that would tell us that we have made it to Idel." Buckner said.

"We are way out of our league right now, and I don't even know what to believe about this. We don't even have a clear idea about what we are going to be doing from here on out and that kinda scares me you guys. Who says we will make it out alive in the next …" Sicily said before stopping.

A calm had come over her as she spoke, it seemed that the spirit that was within her had gave her a bit of relief to her thoughts of fear. Immediately she began picking out sticks and twigs to add to the fire. The guys could tell that it was the spirit because a certain calm had come to them as well as they too began to look for more sticks and twigs to add to the fire. It was almost that easy that they had forgot about the spirits that took a bind to them and who had accompanied them in this long and dangerous journey. We can go out looking for fish at the pond near here, as the spirits had enriched the souls of the three scholars they knew things that they normally wouldn't have.

"We can do this…" Sicily said before sighting a man walking a path to them.

"Hello there," the strange man said.

The group was shocked to see anyone around this time of day yet they weren't too afraid for that matter. They stood on an open road that led way to the next city and they knew that it would have been only a matter of time that they may see someone.

"I apologize if I have startled anyone, my name is Justin and I live not too far from here." Justin said.

"It is our pleasure to meet you Justin but what are you doing out so late at night, shouldn't you be sleeping around this time?" Sicily asked.

"At least it would seem this way," Justin replies. "I had some business within the city and I live just a few paces farther from here in a home that my family had built before they had passed. I stay alone and I spend a lot of time within the far city to keep myself kept with the basic essentials. Sorry if I'm not what you may be expecting about this time. Someone in your field may figure that they could be saved and taken to shelter for rest of the night. Yet I can offer it if that is what you may have wished for." Justin said.

The group of scholars had looked over one another in the shear belief that their prayers have been answered for a first time coming. The interruptions gave them an opportunity to be settle comfortably, at least for the night. The group of scholars agreed that they were unbearable sleeping situation and would enjoy a night's stay at the home as the man simply led the way. The walk wasn't far and the pond was right around the way of where they were to stay for the night.

"And here is my home," Justin said entering into the door.

The home was less than average and showed an adequate amount of space. It was filled with multiple rooms that they all could sleep in alone and a kitchen that spanned more than a third of the first floors space. It was a humble home, which is at least what Sicily had come to say about it. Together they decided not to get too comfortable and to remember that they were only passing by. In which Buckner had added to say toward Justin, whom in return had assured them that things were just fine.

A conversation had arose and Justin was the head of topic as the scholars tried to figure out why he was so far away from either Idel or the far city. It was odd that his home was smack dab in the middle of nowhere and that he was perfectly comfortable about it. With less to say, Justin wasn't an odd looking guy it was just suspicious to be so far away from the surrounding establishments that thrived with people. For some it wouldn't have been mistaken that he was just a loner yet Cash and the crew could tell that he had an odd way of accepting his life. About an hour had passed and the crew all knew that it was time for them to get some rest.

The three all took to a room and rested for the midday to come. During the time of rest Cash was deep in sleep when he could hear the silent yelps of another coming to him. Help, help me please and please wake up. As he did it was odd to notice that he was tied to the bed and Sicily was stirring in her yelling.

"Help, help me please, Cash, Buckner. Please help me." Sicily cried.

What could he do he was hog tied to the bed post and unable to move around. He was helpless to hear the sound of her cries coming from afar. Cash was clueless to think as what had actually had taken place and why he had been tied up in the first place. To have come this far in the journey he knew that the man was odd for a reason and it was clearly because he was a threatening enemy. The cold morning breeze rushed through Cash like a naked body in the wind. The building held no windows so it had to have been the front door. Immediately he knew that Sicily was on her way in becoming gone.

With a thought in mind he began shifting once again with the shape shifting spell as his arms shifted larger than the beds post, tearing through the tightly wrapped rope. He took the time to retrieve his sword and upon entering the hallway he met with Buckner who too had his bow ready to commence for battle.

"He took Sicily." Cash said.

"I bet he did, let's go." Buckner responded.

They ran from the forged wooden home as fast as they could in search of Sicily, but she couldn't be spotted anywhere. They searched a small area near the sides of the home in order to look for clues yet they couldn't come up with one. Like a sound of something being torn, her voice opened up through the open woods and said, "Please come find me."

In a dead sprint they took off in search of her, heading back south toward Idel. Why has this happened and were they the only ones that this had happened to? These were the questions that ran through their minds in midst of the search, how could they ever find her? Luck pursed its head when they waited for another clue when a voice veered from a distance of only a couple of feet.

"At last a virgin sent to me from God that I will be able to have my way with." Justin said.

"Please, let me go." Sicily cried.

Cash and Buckner heard her voice and wanted to take a stealth approach to her rescue. In a crouch they traveled through the tangled woods in a slow creep.

"I will never let you go, for you are the hopes of my pack. Do you understand what is going to happen to you? Do you understand the purpose of virgin female blood and how it cures the daylight rest that most wolves sustain? Not too many do understand yet nobody really cares and now I may have my way. For years others sustained in only believing that vampires may cure their age with virgin blood but us wolves suffer a similar defeat. I, myself am the truth of that matter since the first time that I had sustained virgin blood. My body had counter-reacted in a way that I am able to obtain full control of my feral veins that flush a thirst for whatever that I may please." Justin said.

"No I don't know, then what will you do with me?" Sicily cried.

"You will be the bearer of new life, for a lifetime to come my new pet." Justin said.

Cash and Buckner were really close to the pair by this time and they could see the man kneeling over Sicily in his attempt to collect blood from her. He carved a piece of her flesh with the use of his knife, tearing into her skin. Blood rushed from the wound in a thick dark red color that flowed like thinned honey as he collected it inside of a small vial.

"At last the life that all feral may wish for has come, and you my lady will bare its fruit." Justin commented.

"Get away from me you creep, I'll scream again." Sicily said.

"Don't count on your help, I bet your friends are a bit tied up right now!" Justin laughed.

"Not anymore Justin, let her go." Buckner said.

"Ahh, spectacular a few others to see a revolution at hand. Too bad you won't be around to see it." Justin said.

Cash and Buckner weren't too concerned by what Justin was commenting, instead they rushed the man. Cash speared the man knocking the blade from his hand and forcing him to the ground. Buckner on the other hand had readied a bow to take a shot at the unjust man. He suckled his bottom lip in an attempt to get a clear shot of the man.

"No sense of trying, I got you in my paws." Justin said in a radical tone.

The man began shifting, shifting into the true being that he solely was. While his bones crackled, he screamed severely to the pain that his transformation was giving to him.

"You will know pain." Justin said.

The man's mouth protruded and fangs grew from his jawline. It wasn't long before the man was a beastly wolf, a feral of the wild. The robust wolf had already caused Cash to back away from his large frame in fear that he would be torn by its oversized body. Nothing could keep Buckner from taking a shot at the beast that now stood at its full height. It roared ghastly in hopes of provoking fear in the scholars who in returned showed no fear. 'Zip' an arrow flew and grazed the left shoulder of the wolf causing it to approach in a speeding craze.

With his sword drawn, Cash attempted to stab the beast with a thrust that was taking straight forward by the wolf. Justin took the sword into its body further so that he may get closer to Cash in an attempt to tear at his skull. The scene was moving in a quick formidable fashion that Buckner barcly had time to send a second arrow to the beast as it struck him in the right shoulder. *Roar,* the beast lashed out in upset of pain that it back handed Cash, knocking him to the ground. The blade that hung from Justin's side mangled his body as he removed the blade while he held onto the handle he threw it at Buckner.

"Buckner ducked, and caused the blade to get stuck into a tree behind him. No one kept a clear sight of the beast that he had vanished before them.

"Are you alright Sicily?" Cash asked.

In pain from her wound to her arm she was still quick to answer Cash's question.

"Yes, I'll make it." She said.

Buckner returned to the stuck sword after hoisting his bow, and drew the sword from the tree with a loud *thump* as the suction released the sword.

"Here you go buddy, you did great." Buckner said.

Buckner handed the blade back to Cash and the crew was

reunited once again. Cash took to the aide of Sicily by tearing a piece of his cloak and wrapping it around her wound. The blood then eased its flow and she was relieved from some of the pain.

"I think we should track him down before he gets loose and try to harm anyone else." Cash said.

"I agree, but where would we start?" Buckner said.

"Here." Sicily said while pointing at a footprint.

The print looked as if he was heading back south, deeper into the woods toward Idel.

"Then fine, let us hope that we find him before he begins to harm anyone else." Cash said.

The group took off in the direction of the footprints, with only one hope of finding the beast before he could serve to cause any damage to others. The print trail was long and it took them close to a quarter mile out where they came to a haul at a stream. The group checked the surroundings to see where the werewolf could be. The darkened sky and fluorescent moonlight couldn't bare light through the shimmering water. Cash had exhaled a sigh of contempt since he didn't know where the wolf had taken off to.

"Prepare yourself!" Buckner yelled.

The water shook in a trembling procession as Buckner had notice the change in the way the waters had rippled. From a split view he could see a swelling within the waters. He had held even tighter to his bow and pulled back hard on the string to take aim for the beast. The swell made its way closer as Buckner released an arrow. The distance between him and the swelling was no more than eight feet of distance when he had made his mark.

Argh, a beastly man had yelled.

The group was aware and yet shocked to see that they had not hit the wolf yet another beastly creature, the troll Natu. The waters had fell from another living beast that swarmed underneath it. It had swiped within a lunge forth at Buckner grabbing hold of his head. With a wild swing, Justin had tossed Buckner towards the channels walls. The strength that Justin carried with him was unmatched, as it caused Buckner to hit his head upon a rock on the hillside.

Buckner was unconscious upon being thrown around and Cash had watched from a distance.

"No," Cash had whispered.

With the water following as to the movement of Justin, he walked forward toward Cash. His eyes were open in widened frame as he snarled and lunged to Cash's area. Cash jolted, stammering for his sword before the beast had landed on top of him, pinned to the ground. *Roar,* the beast yelled with the sword crashing through his shoulder blade. Again he had took the sword in to take a better arms reach of Cash. The beast let out a loud yelp before smiling viciously at his conventional reach to Cash.

There was no more hope to be had and Cash was well to his death, when he began to take to the wolf form himself. His bones crackled and his body stretched to the dominant size of the wolf's full form. A decision that had suited him well he had thought to himself. In the wolf's form he would be able to hold his own against a true massive beast. Cash quickly took a bite at Jason's hand as he threw the beast from on top of him with the use of his hind legs. The toss caused dirt to crash around Jason's body causing a large dust cloud to form, encasing him ino a dusty shadow.

Roar, Jason screamed before scampering away into the dark woods. Cash tried to follow him but it was no real hope if he wanted to stay with his group of scholars by the braking of dawn. Instead of chasing after Jason, Cash decided to head back and check on his team. Sicily was just getting up when Cash had shifted back as he walked up to her.

"Cash," Sicily cried. "A wolf again, I see it all worked out. My hero, Cash, hey there is something I've been wanting to do and with all the grave levels of danger that when been through I would say that there isn't a better time than now."

Sicily hugged Cash and gave him a big kiss on his lips. At first Cash hesitated to receive it before he calmed his senses. The two had marinated for a moments time before Buckner had stumbled back into the picture.

"I'm so glad that you two were worried about me." Buckner said.

"Oh, sorry Buckner." They said in unison.

"Forget about it, it looks like we are going to have to look for somewhere new to stay at." Sicily said.

"Maybe, but then again maybe not." Cash said. "I remember hearing Elee and Samhain talking about Natu."

"You mean the troll that I had shot with an arrow? Right!" Buckner said.

"Well right." Cash replied. "Something would be strange if he doesn't have a home of his own yet.

"That could be pushing it Cash." Sicily responded.

"But it may be the only thing that we have to work with." Cash said.

The group of scholars all looked in the direction of the stream to see the troll standing and gazing at them. His redefined appearance made them jump at a first glance yet they knew that if they had to mention Samhain then it could equal to a greater promise of being kept. They had nothing to hold onto as a second or third option so they all agreed that it would be the way that would mend the process of their travel. They stayed tied to one another as they approached the rather large sized overbearing of a mannish being. Once they had reached the edge of the stream they all looked hard and long at the standing troll to only have him stare back without giving a forward action.

Argh, Natu had yelled in anger at his wound of his shoulder. "For what reasons have you laid me with your bow that I now stand here in pain."

Buckner didn't want to buckle under the pressure of becoming the creature's enemy or worst threat so he tried to remain bold. He tried to get Natu to understand that the threat was the creature that had taken off and that he was going to kill Natu with a given chance.

"Is this the truth?" Natu asked.

Both Cash and Sicily shook their heads up and down.

"There was nothing that we could do to stop it either, if it was up to him he might have eaten you for supper and fed the scraps to his pack." Cash said.

Natu pulled the arrow from his shoulder and gave another quick yell for joy. He knew that the wound would heal and that he would make a quick recovery if he paid attention to the wound. But now Natu was really wondering, why the group had spent the time to even come to speak to him? For the sole purpose of his own to collecting money he hasn't come to any understanding of how to accept people into his life. It was the first time since speaking with his maker that he has actually interacted with any opposing life and it was becoming of him.

"So you don't wish to hurt Natu?" He said.

"NO, sir." The group said in unison.

"Then why you have returned to me, what is it that you wish of that makes you come to me." Natu said.

"You see we need your help." Sicily said.

"MY help, my help! You need my help!" Natu said.

"Yes." The group said in unison.

"I don't think that would even be possible for you to ask since you don't even know the great Natu. If I had to think about it I would say that you were after my money and that is all that you want from me." Natu said.

"No that is not it, we don't care about how much money you have." Sicily said before letting out a whimper.

"Ha, ha, ha, ha that would make me laugh if something was ever funny. The great Natu is the owner of this bridge and it cost to get across. Did you know that?" Natu asks.

"Yes," Sicily said. "Our master had told us all about you."

"About me, what could your master have possibly told you about me that could stretch past a weeks' time that I've been born. Who of who at all would speak so dearly of the great Natu." Natu said.

"Anyone, if that is what you are thinking." Cash said.

"Exactly and I have a great deed tending to this bridge that I had made a way for what I can do so far and the world would want to take that from me." Natu said.

Natu began walking toward the edge of the bridge as the water dripping from his clothes created a trail that had softened the soil as he walked. The group followed him as they wished to try to reason with him. It was still turning into morning and they are pretty sure that he could have a place to stay for the moment that could be more beneficial than what they had been dealing with just recently. But the only thing that was blocking that was the effort to getting him to understand the pressure of what was at stake.

"You all speak as if you know me so very well." Natu said.

"Sure, you can say something like that because we serve under the same cause as you do." Buckner said.

"Oh do you really, I was created to take a toll upon this bridge and that is why you are here?" Natu said.

"No. We serve under the same master, Lord Samhain." Cash said.

"Lord Samhain. My master and creator." Natu said.

"Yes Samhain," Cash said. "He told us about you Natu.

"You knowing my name speaks a viable amount of truth to what you are saying. It was as if I had almost already forgotten my name by the time that I had heard it for the first and last time. And the master, is he alright?" Natu said.

"Yes he is well." Cash said.

Cash placed his hand on the wounded shoulder of Natu. He tried not to apply any aggressive amount of pressure to it. He pointed out to Natu that he served the same master and that they should come together in an alliance of the unbalance of power that is taking place between Central, Idel, and the far city. It was as if a new awakening had taken place and the bind that is keeping things in their designated place have finally loosened up once they heard the words coming from Natu's mouth.

"I will help you."

The group cheered and applauded the Troll as they all felt that their lives have been saved. Surely they could have come together and rebuilt a whole city if they had solely wanted to but in what type of time. They were struck with the way of fashion that compelled them forward and were pressed by the time that it would take to get a clear angle of things. The plan was set forth and the group all felt a sense of peace knowing that they were in good hands. The only thing was the construction of knowing how it may feel if it all came to a crashing end that moment.

Cash held onto Sicily as they followed Natu to his home, the wild stream of brush and long branches smacking at them was a great excuse for holding her. At least after just finding out the outstanding amount of feelings that she had for him, he wanted to make every moment count. Buckner trailed the group, he equipped his bow and stood ready for any more of those wolves who wished to take the group away from succeeding. Natu hadn't led them a far travel and they were there in a matter of minutes. He stayed in an average sized oak tree that practically stood on its own roots.

"Home sweet home." Natu said.

Buckner tried to scavenge the tree before he was cut short

by Natu. Natu didn't want anyone snooping around near his horde of money that he had already collected. It was a lot. In any real comparison he had a pile of coins in a large mound underneath one of the tree roots. Buckner knew that the amount would be able to fill at least one large chest. Natu wasn't too hesitant in thinking that anyone would come close to overtaking his coins so he didn't want the chance to arrive.

The group was happy to be alive but now in the moment of despair and confusion. It was great to meet new allies, but yet they still missed being in line and centered within themselves and their thoughts. The playing field was way off base for them to gain some sort of leverage that would prove to be helpful. For what they were understanding now is that this could go on forever, and this is what was going to become of them. Cash on the other hand was feeling as if his life has just began.

~ ~ ~

The morning sun was setting in as the streak of heat flushed over the open sky bringing light to land. The time to find shelter had stormed over and it was clear to see that Maxin and Elee were both safely hidden inside of an old abandoned barn house. The two had been talking all night about what steps to take after noticing that the hope of finding extra help within the far city was out of the question. It had seemed that all was lost and they had to come together if they really wanted to end the war that is raging onward. Then it came from nowhere.

"What do you think those managing wolves could be up to

at the moment?" Maxin asked.

Then a revelation struck like no other, it was almost as if they had forgotten and now she was the keeper of the lost. As far as she was to understand she had a plan to play and it would come together as easily as she had thought about it.

"Maxin, do you remember when the wolves attacked the Political family a few years back?" Elee asked while lying on top of a stack of old hay.

"I can't really forget, it was all over the city for months." Maxin said.

"Right, and nobody had believed that it was a wild pack of werewolves." Elee said.

"True, they all came to the conclusion that they were over large regular wolves just to keep things on a hush." Maxin said.

"Exactly, but for what reasons had they attacked the political family and not any other families around. Something tells me that the families of politicians are hiding something, and I do believe that Jasper is hiding something as well." Elee said.

"Yea, no kidding. I remember when he was a kid and he did nothing but play outside and run around demanding things from the locals. All he would say is that he's going to be somebody and that he should be respected." Maxin stated.

"I know right, know look at the times. I wonder if he already knew what was in store for himself. I mean nobody really knows what they will be doing in life until around the last minute of understanding. I mean once all the cards are actually set down on the table then that's usually when one person would understand more about themselves." Elee said.

"That, for the most part is very true. It's as if you remember all the best parts about childhood and bring them to life." Maxin said.

"And his childhood was a bit quirkier than others. Well not to mention being born into a family of wealth." Elee said.

"That right there is very true. When I was his age back then I was still trying to find myself and never once had I thought about entering the priesthood." Maxin said.

"I know right." Elee said. "I came when I realized the life of crime wasn't measuring up, and I needed something that held a bit more security."

"One thing is for sure, if we both had spent more time researching the place then we too would be able to have the level of skill settings that lord Samhain presents. He's really something isn't he?" Maxin said.

Elee didn't want to speak into her feelings about how she felt about Samhian, because if she had it would be a whole different level of conversation. Instead she let Maxin's statement roll right off of her mind and played back into her thoughts about the politician.

"Yeah, see hey what about the "Night of the Politician?"

Elee said.

"What? Um yes well what about it?" Maxin said.

~ ~ ~

It was pushing closer to noon and things were stirring up in the house of the politician. As the man of the hour had ordained every thought that he would build when he took office, but he was faced with an even greater dilemma. He had reason to believe that he would prove to be the most proficient and sought out individual of all time, even more than the priesthood itself. But for now it would be an understatement for him to quiver at the loss of his big turnout. He was going over his layout plans for the setup of the event and he wanted to be seen by anyone who could stand or walk.

For the politician it would deliver a major viewpoint of him that would open up others to his walk of life. A life that would prove him more favor than any other aspect of realization but yet still forward it onto others living on their personal need. The politician wanted to eradicate the human race and build his army of vampires. He is quite the optimistic type and share no feelings of defeat or defiance at the hands of what could be his big break. Never the less he was to be named supreme in the chain of life as it showed in the forth coming of his dreams.

He thought harder on how he could ease the minds of those who showed no real affection for him or to his ideas and then it struck him. Those who show no favor to him would come to terms of being a hand of slaves during the forum of him being a tyrant to his people. The evil ideas endowed more space of what truths he was really searching for. He vowed for a space of a general assembly that would hold to his way of being as an evil name to the humane races.

Yet besides what he held dear to his own ideas, he still had to make a provincial stand at where he was for the moment. Deviously he contoured the relocating thoughts of taking people and making them understand his way of life. He was so convinced that he was willing to do anything that was at his disposal. The clock was ticking and the man needed a theme, something that would make a marking of what can display a tribute to his party then his eyes rolled fully open and another idea came to mind. *Why not have costume parties?*

Out of all things what could stand against a night where one person can dress to their liking of an eventful evening that he would call Hollows Eve. It was perfect for all of the uncanny thoughts of sorcery that called to the many minds and hearts of others that expelled to their truths.

"Come to me, please my next at hand please listen to what I have to say." Jasper said. "We need a theme for this event and a great one and that is why I have come to a cunning solution. At this event we shall call it Hollow Eve to celebrate the end of October. This ending of the season of summer would storm a new revolution of all party goers and commoners of the land. This event would become national and I would love to hear my name being brought forth through the years to come."

"Perfect sir, and I will make a note of this yet something has come up and I believe for it to be urgent sir. I was told that at least three dozen ranks were slaughtered by the Celtic Priesthood." The second hand man said.

"This is untrue, I have never come to hear of something like this in all my wild thoughts. Who? How has this happened?" Jasper responded.

"Sir the thought is unknown and we would surely believe that Lord Samhain has something to do with it. To me it would seem that he was aware of our move across the land and he made an attempt to stop the suppression." The second hand man said.

Jasper was enraged with anger and fear, was it all true? It was just last night that he had met with Lord Samhain and the accord was all yet peaceful to the thought. If he had thought of overtaking the land from Jasper then it would come as a surprise to Jasper as he well knew of it. There wasn't a thought in his mind that said something as if it pointed to the wolves for a stake at his hopes. The mere dreams of them connecting with another source of dominance wouldn't dare cross them for they too also had Jasper to thank for some of their delightful freights.

"Very well then, we shall be upon guard at my eventful night and hold the priesthood responsible for my inevitable destruction of my followers. They will pay for what has happened and they will suffer. Yet until then we will continue onward as planned and have to our own fun as we wish." Jasper said.

The second hand man heard Jasper very well and was sure that he too would follow in order. He made plans of having extra men to being on guard for the politician's party and that he should see himself there as well. If there was some force that strong then he would see to that they could never break the forces protecting the politician. It would seem that the politician was having his way with the hand at power and it would prove to be one that is in demand.

~ ~ ~

The scholars had just awakened from their naps and were almost forgetful of what had taken place. The wound on Sicily's arm was layered with dried blood and the wounds of the others were still sensitive to the touch. They ached in their attempt to rouse themselves back to life and they sought to begin preparing for the inevitable. The thoughts that this thing could get worse had sprung up in their young hearts at the beat of every second and it still forced a cold thought of resistance to mind. It was becoming harder to build their focus on a win of a battle that they surely hadn't had an idea about.

Buckner was taking the first step in preparing himself as he drew to practice with his bow. A nearby tree was perfect for the onslaught of an aired attack of arrows that flew like birds in the sky. Each arrow took rest in the same three inch circumference from one another creating the perfect circle. It was a major wake up call for the scholar that he tried to hold to his strength as much as he possibly could.

Cash and Sicily were taking things a bit differently as Cash was spending time aiding his girlfriend. He wished the best for her and he wanted it to be known to her that he wouldn't leave her side. Needless to say that the spirits that had consumed their bodies were too lovers of a kind and it warmed the commitment. Agreeing they had comforted one another with countless amounts of affection being displayed and that it was making Buckner uncomfortable. Seeing they weren't what we're causing stress within the young man, it was the fact that he couldn't have the lover that he wanted.

Fear of losing out by no means of having food, Buckner prepared to start making snare traps as he set out to hunt for meals. He was alone in his thinking that the newly acquainted couple and the Troll were at peace with what drove them wild. It was easier said as then Buckner has started taking in with Uncle Joe, the spirit that had consumed him. Thought by thought the two began relinquishing ideas on how to obtain that of what Buckner had really wanted priestess Elee. The spirit of Joe had talked to him, telling him that he was far better than Cash or Sicily and that with his help he could prove his dominance to the priestess.

Buckner was becoming pleased by what he was hearing and wanted to make an effort in showing how he was the one for her. He wanted to prove how he was man enough to carry her and the bridge that she stood upon. He became elated with energy and envy that showed in all of his talents as he hunted. He started out by snagging three bunnies and laying down a deer whose antlers settled like a spanned tree. The young scholar was feeling very confident in himself when he realized that he was going to need some help in carrying the deer carcass to the camp.

The young scholar tried to reason with his peers first and only to find out that they held no interest in the deer. That his fellow peers, they rather they shaved a piece of meat for their worries and feed the rest to the animals of the forest. Buckner wanted more for his accommodation and sought that they would have a greater feast if they kept the whole creature as he went to Natu for his help. The troll was fast away at his post upon the bridge when he heard the approaching steps that he couldn't reason to who it was.

"Aha, who goes across the bridge of the great Natu that I will take a toll for your approach." Natu said.

"Fear not the great Natu that it is I, Buckner and I am here to ask a favor of you. I am here to ask if you will help me with the kill that I have for our meals to come." Buckner said.

Sure Natu was hungry and would love to take a moments rest to fill his hunger pain, yet he sought nothing more than the riches that barreled and the base of others. For Natu didn't want to leave his post for any reason until it was time for him to rest. He was creative enough to catch his own gain upon will and didn't need the help of others. It wasn't time for Buckner to be spiteful; instead it cleared an anguish that he has never noticed with himself. In his eyes he was focused and cleared of any negative thoughts that he would fulfill any necessary desires.

Buckner thought less of the kill that he had and insured himself that it was only child's play to think less of it. He knew that the gain was major and that despite him not being able to carry the carcass that he had come through for his team. He resulted on the idea of leaving the deer for the wild to consume and keeping the rabbits that he caught. Surely nobody would mind, if they did then they would have spent more time hunting than trying to leave him to the just of things by himself. Something different was becoming of Buckner and it was obvious that even he didn't know about it.

Nobody noticed the difference in the serving of food that they hadn't eaten deer and it was just fine. Buckner had given them the action of his sincerity and they hadn't taken it. It would seemed that Cash and Sicily was so worried about one another that they had completely forgotten about Buckner, their one true friend. Despite the level of anguish of what had been, Sicily had awaken from her stern desires of Cash to present to the group that they should spend more time trying to find a way back home. It sounded like the right thing to do, not just because it was heading home, yet it stirred a conflict with a certain someone.

This certain someone was well within the containment of him and wished everything else but it. Why?

Why leave now and the whole just of what he is truly searching for would be lost against his will. His true will is to find love of his own and in due time have the charitable feelings that Cash had settled upon with Sicily. Buckner was relentless to leave Elee alone now in her time of need.

"We're staying until we meet up with the others and that's final!" Buckner said.

Cash and Sicily displayed no form of warmth and didn't want to spend any more time wasting around in the woods. If it came to how they really felt the mission was a waste and they had failed. They had failed in the search of the other temple in the far city and they knew it very well. Yet what was next to come for them while lying stranded in another town that they didn't know.

"We need to get to a safe place and fast, were not going to last out here in the woods! We aren't the type of people who can leave a life behind and start something new in an unknown region." Sicily said.

"Well stop thinking that everything is already over, we still have time and we need to wait for Maxin and Elee." Buckner said.

"Well that is original. Just when I thought you were looking out for the rest of us you turn it into something very selfish. You will never have the priestess and she is well past the needs of you." Cash said.

"You take that back!" Buckner said.

"Never, forget that you have a crush on the priestess and forget the fact that you slept with her." Cash said.

"How can you say that?" Buckner said. "After all that I have done in our training and helping you with yours. How can you say that I've been less than the priesthood?"

"Oh yeah, you been focused on the priesthood and then some," Cash said.

"Just like you and Sicily." Buckner said.

"Just like how I'm going mess up that pretty little face of yours." Cash said.

Immediately Cash swung his fist at Buckner's face, knocking off his glasses as he flew backwards. The scholar tumbled over Natu's bundle of cash and then rolled underneath the tree stump.

"That would teach you some respect." Cash said.

It wasn't long before Buckner had returned to his feet and then began pursuing Cash.

"I'll show you." Buckner said.

Buckner then began casting the transformation spell and shifting into a bear. The process was the same as his teeth protruded from the gorge of his mouth and his arms widened with strength. Claws had grown from the palm of his hand, and before he completed his trasformation, he let out a horrifying *roar.*

"Stay back." Cash said.

Doing what he knew best, he too had shifted into a bear to fight with his fellow friend. The clash was a bit too intrusive for the size of the tree trunk that they had been living in. A large sized paw struck the face of Cash as it sent him barreling from the trunk base and into the wood line. He rolled and rolled until he finally caught a grip to stand up again.

"Stop it you two!" Sicily said.

There was no hope. No matter what could be said the two went at each other like the raging beast that they had become. Cash stretched the base of the tree trunk in order for him to stand and take a view of where Buckner might have gone to. Sicily had noticed the pair of glasses that once rested to the face of Buckner as she picked them up. Cash was gone by the time she had looked up.

Loud roars surfaced from afar and the two could be spotted fighting once again. They circled one another trying to get the best vantage to take aim at one another. The two fitted right in with the scenery and look as if they were normal bears of the wild fighting one another. Roars wrangled from both scholars: as they stood to their hind legs and trying to bite and scratch at each other. Sicily tried to keep the peace, but between the two scholars there wasn't any peace to be made.

Blood began to flow from the arms of the scholars as their scratching began to make their marks. Sicily hoped that the two would resort to reason and finish this with a reasonable conversation, yet they continued right onward. Finally both scholars had taken a hold of each other by gripping onto each other's neck with their teeth. Blood ran a slithering course from their wounds and the two were becoming very tired and worn out. They were exhausted. The two took tired slashes at each other, causing more blood to ooze from their wounds.

"Now look at you two." Sicily said. "How are we going to survive if you two can barely walk."

Both Cash and Buckner than began drawing away from each other, as they turned back into their human forms.

Cash was tired yet he said. "I always knew there was an animal in you."

Buckner was through with arguing and didn't want to respond to what he had said. Instead he decided to take an organic treating to his scars on his arms. Something had to give, he had thought to himself.

Sicily was very worried about Cash when she noticed the blood running down his neck. She wanted nothing more but to have him back into top shape and she knew that he was far from that.

"Here, let me help you with your wounds." Sicily said.

She immediately drew back to the oversized tree trunk and took him back to treat him. She had thought that if she lost him then she would lose a part of herself and she wouldn't know what to do with herself. She took this second to begin thinking about Buckner. They had been friends for years and now this moment was ruining everything. She told herself that they would be together forever and that is what she had hoped for. She didn't want her feelings for Cash to be the reasoning for losing her friend and she didn't want to lose the love that she was receiving from Cash either.

To her she would have kept her secret if she would have known this much was going to happen. But then what, what would have been her moment of truth wouldn't have been at all. She's took in more thoughts and assumed that it was the faith of each other and that they would have to figure this out and become closer to each other than ever before if they wanted to keep their friendship for the lifetime. *It has to be*. She thought to herself.

"So was this just a last minute chance to say that you are happy that I told you how I felt?" Sicily asked Cash.

Cash was at the least worried about Sicily especially ever since he found out about how she really felt about him. It was a lot to handle and he was pretty sure that he couldn't handle losing her for any reason. Since they first met years before it has always been the three of them and they were inseparable. But the last thing he had wanted was to tell Sicily that he loved it when she would approach him. Cash loved it when she would say "Cash, I missed you."

To Cash, she always stood out and he had been wanted to tell her that for years and now he had his chance. There was nothing else that would stay in the way of what he has now and he wanted that to be known. He also wanted to know if she felt the same way and he was getting her response.

"I never want to break the group up and if we are doing that then I don't know what to say about the group then," Cash said.

"How can you say such a thing?" Buckner said.

Buckner was still wrapping bug juice and leaves around his neck to seal his wounds with.

"You act as if I never knew that the both of you would someday become one with the other. It was only a matter of time. I'm your best friend and don't either of you forget that." Buckner said.

"Sure won't buddy." Cash said.

"Too bad you two were stupid enough to tare each other apart to remember that you are friends." Sicily said.

"Yeah, we got a bit out of hand. But I don't think that it will ever happen again." Cash said.

Roughly Cash felt a bit awkward when the spirit of Morgan had spoken to him. He told him that they should stay put and wait for Maxin and Elee before they start making any new plans. The plan was already set by their elders and they should reason to follow them. Buckner had known that all too well and it seemed that he had assumed leadership control of the group for once.

~ ~ ~

"I have to hope for the best." Samhain said.

He was in his quarters when he seemed to take on accounts of the same thoughts about the group of scholars and priestess. For sure he figured that they were in extreme need of help and there was nothing that he could do about it. Everything had now seemed different and the priesthood was coming to a challenge that they might not be able to handle.

"I can still remember when I started this priesthood." Samhain said.

"What about it can you tell me?" Genesis said.

"A lot. That is if you care to hear about it?" Samhain said.

"As I am here I would like to hear the most of what is to be said." Genesis said.

Samhain began telling Genesis of how he sought out the strength of the youth and how he wished to sustain the beliefs that people had held in God's name. It was then when he tried to bare that he was higher in life than any normal priest and that he portrayed black sorcery in the reasons of his unknown. It was a question to even him. If God reasoned by the use of sacrifices and accepting the willful as they were then why wouldn't he be any different? How different would it been to come closer to God by one's self and create a full priesthood within his honor.

The backdrop was short and full of esteem that Samhain let it be known that it was everything to him. He started his life as a teen being a high believer of God before he rose as head of his own priesthood. It was a special kind of priesthood that takes the acts of life into its own hands by the stories of war. Sure it may take some time to think about yet the bible had been very specific about war in and by the name of God.

To Samhain it pasted a true level of ideology and it tested

the rights of man and woman alike. He was sure that he had won without reason. He had won a battle that rages and that he would be prepared for in the near future to come. With only himself Samhain had thought that the battle was a bit more satanic than he would even imagine. The presence of the wolves would serve to prove that the last is yet to come and he sure had hoped to outlast that thought. Genesis applauded Samhain for his level of rethinking of all the glory in the world; he said that he deserved it.

"Glory to you for your works: Lord Samhain. Glory to you, priest Samhain in the name of the father." Genesis said.

It was time to go back to the day's lesson plan with the scholars and Genesis wanted to see things first hand. It was an optimistic moment that Samhain reluctantly agreed to the occasion. The remaining scholars were all gathered in the main sanctuary composing thoughts and theories with one another. The chatter was an average and they were excited about the day. They just finished eating oatmeal and sausage and had their fill for the morning.

"Now it is time to come together my students," Samhain said.

He managed to get the scholars to quiet down before beginning to speak of the lesson for the day. He wanted to make an impression on Genesis and for him to do so he figured that he should go all out.

"Today class we will be observing how to conduct fire. I

know, I know you already know how to make fire." Samhain said.

The class responded. "Yeah."

"But this my class is something new. It is even harder to consider if someone is weak minded about conduction and should be taken into consideration." Samhain said. "We first argue the fire. Then we ask for fire. This will take a lot of mental connecting with the element as is."

Genesis wasn't too sure of what to say as the darkened room lit with the rays of heat that emitted from Samhain's hand. It was beautiful yet scary in the same sense that he didn't know if it was real. But by all means it was all real and that is what had scared him. Samhain's voice aired in the back of his head as he heard him say, that is why it is a blessing from God. Now Genesis was questioning what he ever knew about God as he knew it.

~~~

They were passing and Maxin and Elee were fast asleep before they were abruptly awakened by a startling and loud noise. It was as if someone was using magic to cause loud bangs to startle them out.

"Elee, Elee do you hear that?" Maxin called out. "Elee!"

The loud bangs were stirring a frenzy with Maxin that he rose to his feet to try to take a look at what was going on. From the way the frozen heat came from the sun's rays he was stuck trying to see anything. Maxin reposition himself on top of a stack of old
~~~

hay to see what was going on when he realized that they were under attack.

A woman crowded by a group of men stood readily to attack the barn as they took axes across the base of the barn. It would seem that they were trying to flush them out and coming so close to succeeding. Next an arrow with fire upon the tip came rushing through one of the open windows and crashing into a haystack.

"Elee! Awake!" Maxin yelled.

"We know you're in there, come on out and surrender or else we would be forced to flush you out." George had said.

But it was already too late and the barn was on fire.

"I said hold all actions." Constable George said.

The woman came close to him and said, "They have to pay for what they have done, they have to pay."

"Lady, you and this mob has got to go." Constable George said.

The crowd of people were growing louder and louder with their chanting and ranting onward about killing the priest and priestess. They began calling them the awkward six and wanted to see them all dead. On the other side of things Maxin had finally wakened the priestess as she watched from the slit in the angle of the barn the massive group of people who sought to end them.

"What do we do now its minutes until sundown and we are

trapped in a burning barn?” Elee said.

“It’s one thing to worry and another thing to spot out the obvious, we have to wait it out and see what will come of this.” Maxin said.

“Nothing, but the death of us is going to come from this and that will be the last of the priesthood if they ever find out who we really are.” Elee said.

“That is why we will flee at the breaking of sunset and take to the woods.   Then we can manage to find another wagon to take back home.” Maxin said.

“You all aren’t going to get out of here alive and that’s on my own life I declare that I see the end of yours.” The woman shouted.

The crowd was encouraged and enraged. What was going to happen to the unlucky pair? Would they surface to being burned alive or was the massive group so far out for blood that they were going to kill the pair? The telling was becoming indescribable to the priestess and she wasn’t going to stand for too much more of it. The sun was drawing near full sunset when another arrow with fire was launched into the barn and the crowd cheered happily.

The smoldering smoke launched the two priests into a frenzy as they searched for the nearest exit.

“It is not time!” Maxin said.

“Then I will risk my life to be taken by sunlight than to die of this.” Elee said.

"Soon, real soon." Maxin said.

The lit horizon began to darken as the shade of time had begun its fulfillment. And then the mob began tearing at the broken chard wood of the barn.

"Kill them. Kill them all!" They chanted.

The smoke exited the barn with excess speed as the sky was lit with a greyish, darkened black color. The heat rising to a peak as it suffocated the air from their lungs and like alone that willed the life of the fire.

"Can anyone see them? Can anyone see them?" Someone from the crowd yelled.

The barn was almost fully charred and torn from the fire yet through it all nobody could tell if anyone had made it out. The group stayed their throughout the night for the heated coals of charred wood to smother itself in into ashes. The wild mob was sure that was the end of the awkward six. The only difference was that they had no proof of the ordeal. It was still early in the night and nobody was willing to take the wait so the mob had begun to dissipate as the night went on.

Nobody stayed behind except for the estranged woman that started the mob and she was persistent. The shuddering smoke still arising out of the ashes, yet she wanted her proof as she searched beyond the rubble. She wanted to make sure she knew if they were still alive. Across the horizon a flickering light could be seen above the trees as the shimmer faded away in the dark. The woman had keen eyes and could see the light as it faded out.

The scholars were tired from their early morning rising that day and started to feel tired out from the entire ruckus. Natu himself was still at work at his bridge and it left more space for the teens to stay in. Fast asleep the group would have no chance in acknowledging the difference in the time, the difference in exemplifying their hopes of heading home.

"Were could they be? It is our duty to lead them back home and we are even more clueless as to where they even are." Elee said.

"That is mostly true though we need to take in the possibility that they could be in Idel, it's the closest place from here and they could already had found a place to stay for the night." Maxin said.

"Not without money, the money that I carry for all of us is still with me and they may have ended up in the woods somewhere," Elee said.

"That is something to consider yet we still need to factor in that they are here for us and wouldn't leave unless they had word on doing so," Maxin said.

"For the faith of the priesthood I would hope that you are right," Elee said.

It was as they were just speaking that they had just passed over the oversized tree that the group of scholars had stayed in and now came closer to the bridge of Natu. From the far view of the sky they could see a large-sized man standing midway of the bridge.

Before speaking Elee came to the premising thought that maybe they had come in contact with Natu and perhaps he would know what has gone on with the scholars.

"Look Maxin, I'm going down," Elee said.

She took the time to climb down a group of trees to settle closely to the bridge of Natu. She stood just a few trees away from the Troll and could see him in the midst of the night with her keen sight.

"If we have to search anywhere I'm sure that we can start right here." Elee said.

~~~

The scholars slept with great intent to fully rest as they were slumped over one another and unable to really move around. Cash and Buckner were wrapped with tree leafs and bug juices to soil their wounds for healing. A small fire would have been great for the late night cold yet they scholars didn't want to risk the chance of being seen or even setting the tree on fire. Throughout the makeup of the night a gentle voice could be heard calling out.

"Buckner, Buckner." The voice repeated.

The calling streamed continuously and then even louder until the person was closer to the base of the tree that the scholars were staying in.

"Buckner, Cash, Sicily." The voice cried out.
~~~

Looking into the base of the tree a body could be seen sleeping under one of the large elongate tree roots. The person approached the body and began shaking at it saying, "Wake up it is time to leave."

Buckner immediately awakened by the voice that he knew too well, it was Elee in her attempt to round up the group of scholars. It was time to go and Buckner had understood that as he tried to put avoid eluding to his caring. He immediately withdrew to Cash and Sicily as priestess Elee noticed the wrapping of leaves placed all around the neck and arms of Buckner. She could tell that it was something that they probably didn't want to talk about and so she never brought it up.

"Can you make more of that stuff?" Priestess Elee asked.

Buckner finished rounding up the gang and then they were on the way. It would take a couple of days on foot to get back and they were up for the challenge. I believe that they would have done anything to get back to home. The group didn't waste time saying goodbye to Natu, instead they headed straight out for the open road.

~~~

Genesis was alone when he was approached by Samhain; he wanted to speak to him. Samhain wanted to make sure that Genesis was prepared to agree to becoming a part of the priesthood and that he would join as an official Priest. It was quite clear to Genesis that Samhain had wanted a lot of him and it was more
~~~

than he thought he could bare. Samhain made it clear as well that he had wanted Genesis to take over a different type of task. Instead of fighting or using sorcerer magic he could be used for his natural talents of speech.

Samhain wanted Genesis to become a priest and to lecture the word of God to the scholars. He figured it would be an act of literacy and teaching other than being a bountiful individual like the other priest. He assured Genesis that the word of God had been forgotten and the people would need to understand that the biggest burden ahead of them would be the one that they had forgotten about.

It was becoming clear to Genesis that he was being used as a watchdog, the eyes behind the scenes that kept the perspective in shape and he didn't know if that was what's being asked of him. To him though it sure felt like it. He figured that he would do the relating with others before they would realize the militia of sorcerers being held on board. If it was true then was it really lying to the people about how they worshiped God? Were they staging a story to corrupt the people with a group of vigilant youths who contain abilities that most people would only dream of.

Despite the questioning with himself, Genesis knew that an awkward moment would present itself one day and that he would be right in the middle of it all. It wasn't enough to say that he may still have a faith that needed to be dealt with on a spiritual level. It had been a while since Genesis had partaken in any church events and now he had a full ride ahead of him. He didn't want to linger around having Samhain to wait upon him so he told him that he would think it all over. He had to create some space for the act that would change him for a lifetime.

Samhain was sure that the younger man would come to being on board at some point in the future so he didn't address his manner of thought. Instead, he embraced it and told him that the time that he was looking for was with him and may be used to his will. He was optimistic of the young man who was finding out that Samhain had him in his way of life and said that it would suit such a man. But would it at all really suit Genesis? Was Genesis being taken to start a new track of living or had he been taken captive for a sinister group of Satanic individuals?

The reality was too much at the moment and both men knew that very well, yet time was coming that a choice would have to be made. To change an outlook and start over new or be taken by the damnation that was stirring in the distant future. Samhain came to Genesis and assured him peace at the end of his discord and that the journey ahead of him was meant to be by God alone. Even though he was unsure about this idea of his faith and the reality that beheld it; Genesis took what he heard very passionately. It would be a choice not offered by a regular lifestyle that would change his perspective of life and love.

Genesis began to think about Ambrose and how she would be affected by all of this. She was the main reason as to why he left Idel in the first place and she would remain a top reason of why he would choose no other way. He told Samhain that she would have to be the first to know about his life choice and that they would share an enjoyment through it all. His commitment to Ambrose would have to reign higher than anything else; he counted made sure to say. Samhain nearly laughed as he gave a brief chuckle. He told Genesis that in the eyes of God that he was to be first in line of any ordeal and that is what needs to be taking place.

At the end of the conversation Genesis was feeling confused of how to love, or to the idea of what respect had actually meant. It would be respectful to praise God before his wife yet he knew that he hadn't loved God for anytime longer than he had loved Ambrose. The situation was stirring a dilemma in his mind and he was feeling lost by the act of deciding. He would have to place Ambrose second in his life and he wasn't too sure of how to do that. How can Genesis make such a dramatic change? The night was finishing and it was time to rest when Genesis had seen Ambrose. He wanted to tell her the dilemma that Samhain had questioned him with.

They sat up for over an hour before taking rest and he was practically confused all over again. He didn't want Ambrose to think that he didn't love her because she wouldn't get most of his attention. He began to feel a subtle low about himself for justifying what God was ruling. Genesis had a level of disbelief that he held for what was in store for him and what was to become of the livelihood that was said to be set for him. Genesis had let what he talked about settle within him and starting feeling some relief for what he was thinking and he asked himself, why he was running from God?

It wasn't too long before Genesis and Ambrose had actually had a chance to fall to sleep. Genesis had begun continually having a complex list of thoughts that ensured his arrival. A large pack of wolves had begun chasing him and in his travel of running from the pack of feral wolves he resolves the issue by displaying the hands of God against them. The omitting light of truth that ruined the fleshy steed of the pack diminished in his awakening. Why did he have such a weird dream?

A couple of days had passed when Sasha finally returned. She was rugged with the scent of outside and slightly capped off with dirt from her hands and face. It was a good thing to see her so the others had thought and it was a bit weird to see her without the other scholars with her. Samhain was seething with anger once he had noticed that the scholars hadn't returned. He had noticed that he couldn't get a straight answer from Sasha about what had taken place and it worried him. She continued with saying that it was all a bust and that the priesthood at the far city was no more.

She was reluctant to tell him what she had come to think about in the wake of finding the vampires that had stormed them upon their arrival at the far city and it was for a good measure. She knew that it would bother Samhain and that it would cause frenzy with the scholars. The other thing she knew was that they may not really be ready for what was in store for the priesthood, another thing that she wasn't really prepared for either.

Samhain kept his peace with the priestess and gave her time to bathe and rest in this giving time. He needed her at her top condition so he refused to bash her in doing a bad deed by leaving the scholars behind. Though, Sasha was so sure that nothing else would take place in the time to come. Not from what she understood from the witches eye, the orb that told all future truths. She was going to take a risk that not too many would and it would have her life for it.

Sasha met back with Ilam and gave him her best return greeting she could by showering him with hugs and kisses. She missed her husband and it was emotions that showed it. Genesis stood aside of watching the two meet again. He knew he could have moments just like it when he thinks of how to embrace Ambrose. It was sad to hear about the destruction of the other priesthood and that had him worried a bit. Maybe it worried him too much that he went back to Samhain.

That evening was quiet to say, so quiet that you wouldn't have been able to tell that anyone was even there. At least Sasha wasn't. Sasha and Ilam took to the city for the wee hours of the evening and nothing had been heard of them. Samhain was regrouping what he was to think about the incident that had gone on in the far city and was becoming very frustrated. How would this event that is supposed to clash actually take place? He had thought to himself.

Nobody was prepared for anything to come but it was the faith that they would prevail that kept them stronger. Strength was something that they had in numbers and they were short a few others to keep them in that instance of near faith. The purpose of the priesthood would be keeping the peace and now they seem to be the culprits of a peace that doesn't involve them. This ongoing trial was becoming more dangerous in and of itself. Something was soon to come, but when?

Samhain was preparing for another sacrifice to influence his faith in the father and to his priesthood. He was in the basement of the sanctuary. It held a sliver of corridors and rooms that was off limits to the scholars, it was then when he noticed a difference in the way the spirits would console him. They weren't as bent as to picking or taunting of him. No, instead they were there to appreciate his presence. On a usual basis they would scold the man when he comes to make his burnt offerings yet they yielded at the beckoning of his draw to action.

He had bought a small baby goat that morning prior and had spent his time in preparing it for his sacrifice. Nattuck had attended the ceremony so that they both could share in the hope of attaining God's peace. It was short and quick and held no sense. The completed the blood sacrifice as Nattuck skinned the remaining lamb for the meals to come. Samhain was pleased by Nattuck. He had been by his side for many years.

Together they had completed many task and sacrifices. He was well trusted by Samhain. In fact Samhain trusted him so well that he asked him to attend the politician's event in his place and that he wanted to give a peace offering to Jasper himself. Nattuck was charmed and delighted to complete the task for Samhain. To him he would be doing what he's done for years and that is serving others.

Two nights away only was the 'Night of the politician' and many people would come to see it through. The only hope from now on was to obtain peace from what has happened and to ensure that nothing else would come of it. The priesthood alone was too comfortable with taking its fair share of not having to commit to any serious threats yet, only if they had to.

<p style="text-align:center">~~~</p>

Another night had passed when the priestess Elee had entered into the sanctuary with her body wrapped in leaves and bug juice. It was a sight to see Samhain had thought well to himself. His most loved priestess had finally returned safely with the scholars at hand. She was undoubtedly his most prized piece because of her new life that he thought so well of her.

"Priestess Elee at last you have returned to me and the priesthood." Samhain gestured.

At last for the most part to be held, she grabbed hold of Samhain and gave him a long sultry kiss. She was more pleased to see Samhain than he would have ever thought. Yet Samhain was more shocked than pleased with her kissing him. He had always wanted to keep their lives at a more professional level and kissing was the breaking point.

"I doubt I would have survived if I had not thought so much about you Samhain. Over the years I always dreamed that I would have my time with you and this was something that had to open me to the option. Well, we nearly died and all I could tell myself that we have not even met yet." Priestess Elee said.

"Listen, priestess and listen well. I do care for you and I only want you to understand that our relationship is strictly professional and nothing more." Samhain said.

Shunt by his harsh words priestess Elee tried to act as if it meant nothing more to her. She knew that if she really wanted to obtain peace she would have to leave things as they are. She withdrew from Samhain and returned to her quarters. The scholars on the other hand were more receptive, as they approached the others of the priesthood.

"How was the journey?" The other scholars asked.

"Dreadfully tiresome." Sicily said.

Sicily was clinging to the arms of Cash and they kept hold of each other as they walked back to their quarters. Buckner was hesitant in delivering himself to the others, he felt a certain disdain for his pride. He tried to keep up with the walk that priestess Elee had on her way back to her quarter. He watched her undress in her slit darkened room where he fantasized of her once again.

"What do you want." Priestess Elee said.

The door catered to a shadow that disappeared when she spoke.

"Don't, Buckner." Priestess Elee said. "Comeback to me."

"I wasn't doing anything." Buckner stated.

"Your not doing anything, or anything much. It would be something easy to say for just simply gazing at someone and you have been doing much of that. Even in the stage coach ride I can feel your eyes hovering all around me. Why do I amaze you so much?" Priestess Elee said.

Buckner was shocked that he had been found out. If there was only a way for her to see things the way that he does then she would just listen and accept him the way that he was. But it was only what he had hoped for. He was sure that she was about to scold him for being so close to a pervert. He entered the room and closed the door.

"If I tell you then you would think that I am crazy or even offensive. I have always had…" Buckner started.

"You had feelings for me, feelings so strong that you tricked me into being with you before my untimely death." Priestess Elee said.

Buckner was struck cold at her words he didn't want to cause an altercation for any matter. She was surely aware of his motives but wasn't displaying any anger about it. Why?

"I haven't done anything wrong." Buckner said.

"Then I shall hold onto this truth my love. And forget that anything has happened." Priestess Elee said.

Buckner was shocked when she called him her love. It was

all that he had ever wanted and it sure was what he had enjoyed. But how? How did she seem to know and yet not really care at this point? For all Buckner knew she was madly in love with Samhain. He was surprised at the thought.

"We all may have a secret or two and mine are just as even as yours are. Do you think that it would make things better by the way that you had blinded yourself with your own selfish thinking. You came to me as Samhain, and you don't have to admit it. Just listen. I am with child, a child that you will someday call your own!" Priestess Elee said.

"What?" Buckner said.

Was it even possible to make a child with a vampire? So it would seem that she wasn't a vampire when the child was conceived yet the truth is in the action. Buckner had a revelation of things by his selfish thinking and it would become part of him.

"Yes. Of all things you are a handsome man and I too believe that this child is a sign for a new hope. I hope for you and myself. What do you think of that?" Priestess Elee said.

Buckner grabbed hold of the priestess and he held onto her tightly. What had he done? They just spent a night fighting the pure differences in each other which they are trying to expose and she was adding to the perspective by telling him that she was carrying his child. The perspective that the only difference in the other vampires is that they weren't his own child.

"Then what are we going to do?" Buckner asked.

"Protect your child Buckner!" Priestess said.

It would seem that everything was in full perspective when Nattuck took the chance to ask Genesis and Ambrose if they may escort him to the political event for the night. Ambrose was already prepared that her and Genesis were already going to attend. They agreed that it was fine to attend as a trio and that it would prove to be enjoyable. The plan was set and the group was prepared to leave.

Ambrose wore a peacock feathered mask that was light blue and had a stubbed black nose. With that she wore a sequence light blue dress. Money wasn't an option for them yet they always carried enough for their troubles. Genesis preferred that he be a politician for the event. He thought it would have been good for the turnout applause. Nattuck went as himself so that he could rub the esteems of the priesthood as being notable individuals who respect the accord of politics. The festivities looked extravagant.

A separate set of perimeter lighting was setup around the encampment of the festival. It was a blue color that gave into the arena lights seamlessly. The event was enjoyable to just walk around and have fun playing at various crafts. People could be caught enjoying themselves as they walked around the city streets. Ambrose spent her time tossing balls at a stack of wooden cups at one of the booths. The priest and Genesis had no real intentions on playing all the games; they were really snubbing Ambrose for all that she would like to do. It was almost like a second honey moon for the couple and things were running smoothly.

Time had gone by and Ambrose had won almost five prizes

for her efforts at each game that she played. Nattuck held onto a nicely stitched teddy bear for Ambrose because her hands were all filled. Ambrose and Genesis too held items in their hands that would make the memory of the event all the better. Nothing bad could be said about how they were figuring Jasper as a nice well to do type of guy and they held respect for him.

At the amount of appreciation that was built for Jasper they were intrigued that once they saw the man walks over to the stage and beginning to speak to the crowds. Ambrose had noticed it and told Nattuck so that he may in return be able to give his gift to the politician. He was doing it on behalf of the priesthood and it really meant a great deal that he received it. Jasper walked to the stage and said. "Good evening to everyone".

Nattuck continued inching his way to the front so that he could see who he was. From the distance all he could see was Jasper wearing a black cape with a red trim alongside of a top hat. His face was not covered yet it was still kind of hard for Nattuck to see him. The politician continued onward with his speech.

"I am so glad to see the turnout of people here and we are excited to present to the public the 'Night of the politician. In this event, we open up the city to a night of festival activities in our masquerade setting. The turnout seems great and the politicians are happy to hear from everyone. I am grateful that I will keep my term as this city's fair politician and I look forward to what you may have to say. To that extent, thank you and everyone have a great night." Jasper said.

The crowd was excited and cheered the politician onward. It was as if it was the perfect night and the people enjoyed it all. Before the politician Jasper could exit the stage he was greeted by Nattuck. Nattuck had extended his gift to Jasper before explaining who he was. Something was familiar about the man and Nattuck couldn't place his hand on it.

"The great politician Jasper, my name is Nattuck of the Celtic Priesthood and I offer you this gift on their behalf." Nattuck said.

While his hands still extended he offered the small box that Samhain had given him and shared his hope with the politician. From there Jasper grabbed the box and shared his thanks to the priest, when a certain outburst had taken place. It was a woman. The same woman from the barn fire and she wasn't feeling settled in. She began chanting with a smaller group of others.

"We won't take prejudice without representation of us and you haven't given that. I think it's about time that you pay." The woman said.

Nobody had noticed the woman before except for by the group that she had come with. They gave wild stares and snarled at people with a certain uneasiness that would only be accepted by the wild that it entertains. They were meaning business and to this group only Jasper was receiving negative taunts. Nobody had known what mess the group was in or what kind of consequences that it held but they were disturbed.

Next a large wolf dove into the crowd and sent a few people tumbling in the distance. Groups of people began to run into frenzy when another one had appeared from the direction in which the people had just been thrown. Cries and screams had erupted within this crowd and an all-out war had begun. The woman that began the riotous yells stood upon the stage as she took what was left of the disbursed crowd and she said, "To Lucky, you all will obey," as she too had shifted into one of the wolves that roamed the area.

The situation looked awfully bad when more wolves had begun to appear from all sides of the crowd as they jumped over the other groups of people. They ravished all of the people in sight and began their walk toward Genesis and Ambrose.

"Stay back I will protect you." Genesis said.

Nattuck took a defensive position as he was ready to defend himself at will when people began to withdraw from their cloaks airing weapons. A man with a crossbow aimed at one of the wolves had taken arrow shots at a beast when it fell from an arid attack. Others had more weapons in the shape of swords as they drew them and began fending off the beasts. The appearance of it all was horrid when Lucky jumped from the stage in an attempt to catch Jasper.

Something was strange and Nattuck was aware of it as he noticed that the man had favored the one that he had seen in the cave from his journey. Regardless of the account it was a fight being had and they were in the storm of its direction. Lucky ran upon all four of her legs when she raised up to smack Nattuck in the face with her massive paw. She chased after Jasper as he made an attempt to get away and it wasn't before she had pinned him down to the ground.

"At last I will finish what I had started years ago, you shady antagonist. How would I dare have you think that you would get the best of us and this will be it for you?" Lucky said.

Jasper was horrified and he had no real help until his group of followers unleashed themselves as they fought back. It was the wrong string of accounts Jasper had thought as his men began to unveil. For years he had been kept of revealing his vampire brood when one incident had shattered it all. The vampires drew into unveiling their fangs and hissing at the account of wolves around when the wolves began to cringe. At last another bout had erected itself.

The vampires had begun trapping the wolves by pairs of two and taking them head on. As the wolves fought against the whole crowd, the cloaked villagers shed their might as they began fighting against both sides. Blood filled the lot of the city as it flowed from all of the slayed people, beasts and undead alike. Jasper was barely able to get away from Lucky with the greater hope that he hadn't revealed himself.

Sounds of loud roars and screaming filled the surface as the battle continued and the evil that needed to be vanquished carried onward when a wolf had torn a vampires head from his body. The decapitated head rolled to Nattuck were he had sighted the nature of what the cloaked others were wearing. The garb of the priest he had seen and had thought the faith that he led was in reason. He stood in front of his companions and escorted them to an exit from the arena of death.

"Brothers please, lend me a weapon so that I may fight with you." Nattuck said.

The man holding the crossbow goes into his cloak and releases two small daggers that he handed to Nattuck before saying, "We have waited for you brother."

Nattuck knew very well what that had meant and was now fighting aside of a few brethren from the Far city. Ambrose and Genesis weren't in a safe enough position to leave the area so they stayed near the priest. More wolves arrived as they began their pursuit against the league of priest that stood about. The shroud of vampires that lurked around were being slaughtered by both the priest and the wolves at hand and they were turning shorter in numbers.

Whomever was left of the vampires stood aside of the fight as they noticed that Jasper was protected and their job had been completed. The survivors fled themselves so that they could resolve from death by either hands of the battle. What was left were the wolves and the priesthood and the battle didn't look so good that the wolves had begun charging the priest. What had stood as a perfect counterattack now stood as a standoff that peered before their eyes. A line of wolves stood readily to crash down onto the effortless group of priest that had no intent on backing down.

"Brothers we stand to uplift the priesthood of the far city and our pride that has been snatched before us, that we will win this fight." Nattuck said.

He then rushed at a wolf that stood closely to him. Taking a combative stance against the beast, armed with his daggers, he tore the eyes from the creature as it roared with pain and agony. Another wolf had reared upon him and scratched his back with its sharp claws. Upon the act of being slashed, he backswings his arm catching a dagger into the arm of the wolf as he inverted himself to taking another dagger to the upper back of the beast. Nattuck began climbing the backside of the creature before taking a dagger to its head.

The wound that Nattuck had was severely damaging to his ability to walk. The priest was at a near crawl when a group of priest had surrounded him and one began a regain spell. As the sorcery was cast Nattuck stood to his feet. He was revived with great energy that he insisted that he continue to fight. His men were sure that together alone that they may defeat the wolves and they were right. The number of wolves had fallen gravely had they attacked them with full strength then the body counts would be questionable.

The remaining wolves turned hide and decided to live for another day, a day that will find itself. The feeling was all too good and the occasion was the coming of something that was blissful. At the break of this moment nobody would have believed it unless they were there. Even Genesis had his doubts that they came from the event unscathed, or at least bravely wounded. Yet the priesthood stood out to deal the pain to the dowers that had seemed to want to make others suffer.

Suffering was behind the priesthood and it was also behind Genesis as he began deliberating on how he felt. He felt open and loss, loss to Ambrose that he may lose his wife. It was time for Genesis to make a choice and he had known what he was in for, he wanted to be a part of the priesthood.

Central: The Rise of Genesis

I heard a lot of things these last few months, even seen a few things. But the coming of Genesis stood out the most. He has changed as he see himself become a pastor. He was more at peace with himself, a difference from when he first came here. Time changes us all but he was soon coming to another change as well when he came to me.

"Nate, will you join me in service this morning, I need a key of support and you really tend to your studies a lot. I sure can use you around. Maybe you may become a priest in this upcoming of times. So what do you think." Genesis said.

The chattering being heard in the distance from where he stood in the church and the people were speaking louder than him. A great commotion had been taken when a person had been recently attacked by a wolf in the central courtyard. I heard questions arise about to whom or to how this could have happened just under a years' time since the fight at the new annual night of the politician event. People became petrified in leaving the church that they might ease into a state of bitterness in seeing the scolded flesh that was torn from the person in the courtyard.

There wasn't any doubt that the people had felt the terror as to how this could have happened. The remains of those that were killed from almost a year ago still linger in the city of Central. The count is eminent and can be felt with the touch of your very spirit as they had eased around for this time. Nobody heard a whisper throughout the shadowed night's peered gaze, toward how they felt about going out at night. Jasper had tried to pacify things by telling the people that it would never happen again.

Within the first week of the slaughter that no voice was heard crying in the night as people had begun to forget the sheer terror that was the reality for the politician as well.

Sickened the people rung their tears as cries and shouting in the realm of saying that they had felt the holy spirits that coursed around. In and out the church was alarmed. Genesis finished his devotion while listening to the cries.

"Forgive me father but let me stay here in the sanctuary before I will ever enter that reached of a courtyard." A woman yelled.

"Admit it we're going to die down here, just admit it." A

man yelled.

"Holy father you wouldn't lie to me would you. I just wouldn't be able to put up with it. Are we ever going get over the wolves attacking like this? I remember seeing one just over a hedge over a couple of nights ago."

Genesis was taken back about the violence and hadn't really added it to the skeptics that they were to live in faith. Thus a fate that will take them to an expense of the church that they were prepared to fight. With the scholars available to train they people were skeptic about their numbers. All to the same they questioned the wolves in general. Jasper hasn't been seen trying to take the ends of others by his deer meet and greets. No, he has been hidden and playing politician from the background. There wasn't anyone around to back up the take of the early morning attacks. There was an account of someone never returning to his mother's home central as she expected. He hasn't been home ever since.

Central had lost its peace and the church was the only place to pick it up. Who had to deal with all the people that came in on regular basis through the time that had been entertained, Genesis. He was calm by his most and never gave into the cries that would peer. He would tell them to have faith and to be calm. It meant an awful lot to hear those words being brought forward when someone had just been killed. As a selected victor of the bout, by his association to Nattuck, the people clanged to him.

Though they feared to leave the people came to Roth as their core appreciation fades to bitterness. Almost anyone in Central enters the courtyard and cut through the streets to get home and they feared another appearance. After hours of conversing to the help of the priesthood, they had reluctantly agreed. A few of the scholars would take proceed in escorting the groups to their homes. To have been at the hands of the priesthood wasn't just for the people and they knew it well. Samhain's take to society had ripped and the people thrived by it.

The scholars return to the priesthood had poised his mind. Why the attacks? Why now, almost a year ago from the night of the politician? His mind had riddled the tranquility that he wished to provide yet the question had remained, could he protect them? Samhain wasn't just or ever Roth to the taking of others. He was a well minded man that only understood his life as a priest and the world that throttled it.

It was his thoughts that had queued and his mind could not take anymore. He needed to begin a battle situation and he hadn't come to one. Something was tearing at the priest and it was the truth. How would they last?

"We may need to take some form of action sir." Cash said.

"Yes, are we going to do this forever?" Sicily said.

"Either way I really don't mind." Buckner said.

"Alright, we are going to take a meeting this morning instead of training and we are going to devise a plan." Samhain stated.

The scholars were polished with relief. Taking walks in group may become a bit over the top but it would be welcomed with appreciation. Is this really Samhain's place? As a Celtic priest he's taught to defend and delegate for himself yet apparently he was becoming one of the capitals number one fan. Samhain was at a risk of becoming the beckoning that had ran him into priesthood in the first place, his destiny was in question.

He sought less to dictate things upon his own so he knew where he was going to take his peace, with Jasper.

'Knock, Knock, Knock,'

Samhain reigned upon the door of the politician Jasper. He stood for a moment before anyone had answered the door and he wasn't afraid. Nothing compares to the mess of a walk that showed the sun rotted blood that race against the courtyard. A woman came to the door and she was very beautiful as she caught Samhain's eye. He was mesmerized by how charming she was. She wasn't loud and kind of had a shy relic to her. He was touched that he hoped to see more of this woman in his time of needs.

"To you I say, I am in need of Jaspers attention." Samhain said.

The woman was understanding and accepted the priest into the building. It was Jaspers home and the woman had to of been a maid. It was the first time that Samhain had been seen anywhere near the politician's mansion and it was a first that he had a crush for someone other than the priesthood.

"Sir, you don't understand how much the politician would enjoy to see you." The woman said.

"And what is your name ma'am?' Samhain asked.

"Ma'am, I am no ma'am, Madame Jewel if you must know." Jewel said.

"Well yes, this is the first we've met and I would still to keep things a bit normal around here wouldn't you think so." Samhain said.

"Oh and I do priest that is why you were welcomed in the first place." Jewel said. "The politician had been hoping to acquaint himself with you and asked that I give you something. Its inside and I will get it for you if you step in for a minute."

Samhain had done what she asked and stood on the inside of the door of the building, jaspers home. He was a bit touched when he noticed that it had not been decorated with any more than just paintings. Yet it held plenty of paintings of the old politicians who had lived in this very home, Jaspers home. He owned the home through his inheritance and dedicated it to be his political outpost. I guess that would relate to the reason why he had not decorated it .

The silent return of the woman had stirred Samhain's focused when he had realized that she had returned. She walked with a vanilla envelope in her hand as she came down a flight of stairs. He didn't want to tangle his feelings with something that wasn't there, if he didn't have to so he didn't bother the woman. He was only curios to why he hasn't seen Jasper for the mere moment. Jewel was easy going and assured to Samhain that he was sickened with heartache and hadn't wanted to be seen.

He reluctantly accepted the informal addressing and took the envelope. He was sure Jasper would have acquitted some sort of strategy to uphold the peace that was now lost in the city. Jewel was nice in thanking Samhain for his appearance as a substantial help to the citizens and she told him that Jasper was forever thankful for him. Her words resonated to a quicken reckoning of establishment that she asked if he'd be willing to attain the people's safety for a regular basis.

The record of what she wanted was descriptively written in the envelope and she asked that he spend some time on it and decide if the proposal would be something that he can accept. He was sure that he wouldn't have any real choice to the matter if he wanted to keep his own establishment safe. Willing to agree to some extent Samhain asked if it was any question to how long they would have to insist toward the questioned agreement and Jewel responded until the people are safe. It was much as Samhain had feared for his priesthood that they would be on a constant watch with less to protect them. AS far as others are to believe that is what they have trained so hard for.

Evenly as unjust as to the question , would they protect the people, it still was to hold for a greater assortment for the priesthood. They were prepared for a battle if they had to yet they haven't understood the difference if the oppose weren't even acknowledgeable. Sure Samhain may be able to talk his way out of the fight if the oppose was responsible. On the other hand what responsibility had the wolves had other than killing and thrashing. They weren't the type of people to speak to in an altercation.

The dark priest was unsettled on to take his statement so he asked if he could open the envelope. If he opens the envelope he could get a greater idea about what is being taken into consideration for his priesthood. As he opens and reads the official statement that carried Jaspers seal, he realized that his fair share of the duty was to set up defenses for the day time and that the city militia would take defensive positions during the evening hours. How uncanny if the question had drawn any real concerns. The letter was concise and stricken with only a thought that was throwing Samhain into despair.

He was shaken by the letter yet he knew well enough that the concern was well matched.

"Taking a day shift for our safety he asked." Samhain said.

"That would be so, is it a bad idea to question?" Jewel asked.

"No it is not. My expertise is to know that these beasts are up to something and I don't have the clues to understanding what that might be exactly and I'm pretty sure that the hands of Jasper would be enough to help me consort the theories." Samhain said.

"Very well then you agree?" Jewel asks.

"I agree that Central needs help and if my group of scholars is what it would take then I agree to the service." Samhain said.

"This is excellent news and I will be sure to pass it to Jasper." Jewel said.

Samhain gave his condolences to Jewel and thanked her for having him over under short notice. He drew the detail as to what was expected of him and when he could start.

"This blows." Cash said.

"This can't be any worse than the night shift. They are the ones who are really going to have it bad. At least we can see in the distance." "Sicily said.

"Not only can we see yet we might not have enough energy to carry on for the greater portion of the day with all this heat." Buckner said.

The group agreed and noticed that the morning heat was arousing and stirred them a great deal of concern. The heat was taking them by storm and they were becoming fatigued and exhausted. Exhausted because the least of them they wanted to take action to the opposed and extinguish all levels of unjust actions by them. It was the first thing to enter their minds when they heard of this special duty that was set by them. The militia alone would cause the people more money for taxes and the priesthood was the escape route.

Without the greater burden of having to do battle the

groups were pretty excited of how they were becoming used within the city. It was the recognition that settled the excitement and they knew that they will stand out to the commoners that live on Central. Not to say that they stood out before yet it was different ever since of the battle that took place almost a year ago. The night of the politician was underway in a few days and now they would have to attend by reason other than choice. The priesthood scholars were a bit excited especially those who haven't taken a single action against anyone other than training time.

For some of the scholars it was time to unleash all that they had learned and they were pretty excited for that. What could come of the pressure of being killed by an enemy that can take you by the horde. It was now the burden to live that came in the way of how they were feeling. Since last year's loss of the far city they had acquainted ten new priests and two priestesses. They had taken the priesthood by storm and added a high level of proficiency to the skill levels of the scholars. These skills of proficiency would challenge them for a lifetime.

In turn the priesthood was better prepared for action than they had ever been and they were sure that at a given chance that they would destroy any bout. But at the hands of Lucky it was another reason to be afraid and it was more to her that met the eyes. The attack within the city courtyard could have been done by Lucky but it would be questionable to the reasoning that she had no eyes. Her eyes were goged out by the Nattuck when he bore them clean from her sockets. She had not been able to see sense the taking of that unfaithful night.

Even as the group had retreated she was a hassle to her clan that they didn't know how they would care for her. A way of caring that she had thought would become peerlessly simple in a sort of way. Lucky had tampered with the rearing questions of science and sorcery that had led her to the wake of her own logical thinking. Bore from its spacing she takes the witches eyes and settled them within her sockets and now has the ability to see in a light blue array of sight.

The beast that she was is now more of a hassle that she stirs the insight of containing future insight before the act has taken place. She showed a sign of double vision and could apparently be well hidden unlike any before. The biggest question was when will she take her fair share of the prize and harness the end of the priesthood. It would go well for the priesthood to stay away from the troublesome Lucky and stretch their minds else were. But for the contentment of the priesthood, it wasn't up to them anymore to make such a valued decision.

The guard duty took place as normal and the scholars weren't all that very clear if they would have to take any actions against any opposing threats. It would seem that the trim of light was an excess and they knew that the wolves were only capable of changing under the moonlight. At least it is what they had thought. Something strange had took place a couple of months earlier when a group of ten priest had went and journey to the black forest to finish off the horde of wolves when nothing could be found in their air stricken cave. The worst part about it all is that it took place during the daytime and nothing, not a peep.

Cash, Sicily, and Buckner spoke about a wolf that said he had the ability to cast himself off at will and could do that during the heap of a full moon. What intangible webs that we weave when it hit hard and started to make more sense. It was pretty obvious that the wolves had been out of plain sight and it was more obvious that they just might have had a trick up their sleeves. It was something that only time could tell and it was pretty interesting to find out how conclusive that they were.

Hours have passed and no one had come in contact with the priesthood except for some underage kids who possibly didn't have a clue to what was going on in Central. When spoken to, they only wanted to enjoy the day and play around in the open city. For the priesthood it was something that could be overlooked and not stir too much of the focus being that every entrance and exit was being guarded of groups of scholars. The children played for hours as the rising sun hit a climax of heat at noon and the sun made everyone buckle. Soon they couldn't be seen playing near the fountain for they had left the area.

The scholars paid them no real attention as they were focused on seeing more wolves entering and exiting the area. It had been their duty to keep a watch of the area and that is what they had focused on. Yet being the quilt of the day the sun had started to go down and it was time for the scholars to call it a day and return to the priesthood for counting. A stir of words could be heard in the distance saying left, left, you're left right left. It was the militia setting up to start their night shift.

All of the scholars were relieved when they were told that they could leave and that the militia would handle everything from here. It wasn't an upset at the most when the scholars reluctantly agreed and rendered their services. It was time to go home the scholars thought. The groups filed out in their march back to the priesthood and in a quick return they sought for peace.

"Out of all the people in the world why do we have to do this guard duty? It will seem that we have the short end of the stick and are being taken for granted." One hopeless scholar said.

"Yeah we are!" Another scholar responded.

"Well until the city is safe again it is just what we have to do around here and that is that." Cash said.

"We didn't ask for this." A scholar responds.

"Did Jesus ask to be hung for the jurisdiction of his own people." Sicily said. "Now that is a good question to ask. We have our peace here and now it's being threatened and we are the only ones with the will and strength to carry onward with our protection. This is our job for now." Cash said.

The scholars backed away from the argument, there was no way that they could speak on how to maintain their own protection, no matter how much they haven't enjoyed it. It had seemed that it was all coming clear that they were the trail to be tested and only in due time. As the scholars quieted Samhain appeared and gave them a couple of words of encouragement.

"Time is a tale of courage and strength against all people. It takes the courage to continue and the strength to fight through it. Without either we will fail to preserve whatever it is that we wish to keep in life even if it is our own lives."

The soothing sound of Samhain's voice blew over the scholars with a quick burst of easiness as the scholars let their guards down, they knew better than to taint an unquestionable act that involves living.

"We will continue onward." Rudo said.

Rudo was priest that came to the far city yet he wasn't a priest yet until he journeyed into the black forest a few months back. He was one of the oldest scholars whom hadn't reached his peak to say.

"Very well Rudo, it is good to hear from the likes of you. Perhaps we should be able to obtain peace by creating peace with ourselves." Samhain said.

After Samhain gave his speech the scholars all retreated to bathe and eat supper for the night. Nattuck had cooked already and the food smelled very great. The scent of smothered potatoes and beef stew had its' own acquitted just that sent the scholars in a craze. A hardy meal like that would send any group of scholars into a frenzy of peace. The night was something to be obtained as Genesis had spoken with Samhain.

He began telling Samhain how he felt about the turn of events that had alarmed the church. Was it even to be possible that all of the commotion or turn of events would ever change? Genesis was lending that all will break down to nothing but a bitter war right in the heart of the city and there was nothing that they can do to stop it. His level of alarm was transferring to negativity even for a priest it was hard to justify as positive. The conversation didn't negate Samhain to thinking that all was at all lost.

The priest had rooted himself with an elaborative level of positive thinking and wouldn't be devoured by the presence of it. It was then that Samhain had suggested to Genesis that he had begun taking the combative training with the scholars whom had stayed behind in the morning guard. Something like combative training would draw into a spark of interest for living that would contain the level of assurance with Genesis. The thought was a sure way of staying positive that incurred a certain sustainment to being in the arms of the tempter.

If Genesis doesn't think too well for himself in the battle field then he would be lost to himself for the remainder of the wolves living. The only thing to question is how he would hold up without the training and support of the priesthood. Without any question Samhain was breaking into a point in saying that he shouldn't live in fear that it would swallow him with the given chance. Change was coming to Central and it was at an alarming rate that would come to the end of the harvesting wolves.

"I don't think I can get myself past this. Is there even a safety point that we may enter when the night strikes. On a regular basis Ambrose and I would enter into the night to reminisce about the changes that we have come into and we like do so very much. How would things fade for me in a time of need of help." Genesis said.

"We are to be vibrant and vivacious as possible even if it meant changing how you see the night. Life is meant for change and this is a change that would undertake its own meaning. You would give your life just to have a couple of nights sulking away at the stars and moon?" Samhain said.

Neither man had released any idea to the other of how they understood that they felt uneasy and they wanted that to change. Yet the change wasn't a thing that would appear overnight and it was now time to understand that. Samhain took hold of Genesis shoulder and pointed to the altar.

"In many of times this is where people go to ask for help and you noticed that in a standstill this morning. What I can say is that this will never change and that you must have faith." Samhain said.

"Faith, what faith is there when you're being hunted?" Genesis said.

"Faith is still the acquired touch to keep you peaceful and peace is what you will need to combat the foe without any rigid demise. Believe me life is the captive that you are in and you make the rules. You make the rules for all of you should do and protecting yourself is only an agreed term of option that we live by." Samhain said.

Genesis was quiet. He hadn't retained himself to giving in and he wasn't too sure if he was prepared to enter into the truth: the truth that even without the priesthood that he would have to take account all the things that he can do and that is fight. Fight if he ever had thought that the world had any kind of humility for him. It was his last die or need of a thing and he hadn't wished for it.

"What you say makes complete sense and I need to understand that life is my bordering shell of a thought." Genesis said.

"A shell that you stay in for quite some time until something urgent comes lurking." Samhain said.

A quiet gust of wind rippled in through one of the windows as the room faded to complete silence. Nobody was prepared for what was next.

"Lord would you teach me to fight?" Genesis said.

"That is all that I have been waiting on my son." Samhain responded.

The order had been adjourned and the plan was made. Genesis was to begin taking classes as soon as the morning. Time couldn't have moved so fast that it almost would have been missed about the account of Buckner and Elee. Alone silent in her quarters Elee could be found being tempted by the father of her child whom she had named after him. Buckner had taken more than he could fill and was losing patience with his new love child. Young Buckner, the child that raised many of questions to their parents and still to the world that harnessed it.

The baby must have had an adverse reaction to something because it was growing at an alarming rate. What could be said was that he was healthy and strong yet it took another direction in the growth department. At a mere two months of living the child was the size of a one year old and could walk on his own. It was weird to see but was still obvious that something was very different about this child. The depiction of the child was causing Buckner to go hysterical in his time in his presence. In the eyes of Buckner he had stormed onto a child that was elaborate of the grace that God had delivered.

"At his age he is walking and even by then he would be talking, why he graces us with his presence. This is my child and I love him as I do his mother. Nothing will be able to break this bondage of my family." Buckner said.

"Nothing you say." Elee said. "What if he becomes too much for you and you have to give him a life that is different from what you are used to."

"That shouldn't have to become a problem. If he wasn't yours or mine then he wouldn't be a part of this priesthood either. You see by that, the priesthood is our bond and they are everything to us. So this would make a mark in history that we have made such a beautiful joy." Buckner said.

"How can you say just that. This child wouldn't even be able to stay in the same place as the rest of the children. I'm pretty sure that it would make a whole lot of difference if the parents were officially of the same origins. I wouldn't dare taking any account to say that I like what I have become or even know how to appreciate it." Elee said.

"Well no matter how you put it you are the thing to appreciate and I will make sure that it is your understanding." Buckner said.

The night took onward as the scholar puts away his wife and child for the morning to come and he had enough time to take a two hour rest. It had ended the first night in Central since the attack and the people would be horrified if the priesthood doesn't have a way to encourage living. The morning would jump off into a rugged start when a high ranked soldier had come to the priesthood.

'Knock, Knock, Knock'

Samhain answers to the knock and the man was roughly shaded with contentment. He didn't show any high grade of material upon his clothes except for the two bars that shined on his hat. The man was an Constable and he was pleased to see Samhain.

"Well am I pleased to see you sir. Mr. Samhain capture of death and of all livelihood. I am pleased to finally have met as I praise the accord that the priesthood had come to in stopping the devilish creatures at last year's festival the night of the politician."

The Constable said.

Samhain was amazed that he would become so renowned in the city of Central. It beckoned him that they see a performance in a lifetime. Yet to Samhain he sees a different just to what he had done. It was a disownment to him as to who he was of the priesthood. The accounts of magic, against darkness of life and the intangible reckoning that would take this world. He stood in amazement to the see the account take off and hoped that it wouldn't be his last.

"Why have you come here? It is still restless of the night and the shift isn't ready for another hour to come." Samhain said.

"I have something to tell you sir, and it is about the guard change. We have specific orders to exclude you from the post and take position of the city. This is all that is said in full and I would like to tell you that I am very pleased to meet you sir. But that is all." The Constable said.

Samhain was thrown off for a second. He couldn't tell whether he should flatter himself or tempt the just of what was really at stake. He had dodged the reckoning of what is in store for people. The truth said out by the words of the bible and he wasn't going to have to search in at a peak.

"Well thank you that would give us more time to train and thank you Constable." Samhain said.

He closed the door and didn't speak about how he felt when he heard the battle that took place in the courtyard just above a year prior. If he was only prepared to intervene into the political party then he would have been there to help out. It wasn't his first account of coming into an exchange with these wolves but he didn't want to get so far without his priesthood at hand. He would not last and he knows that is why he came to starting the priesthood at the first place. The accord of his being had been played back and now he couldn't get over it all.

'This time I will be ready and this time I will win.' Samhain had thought to himself. Samhain was preparing himself for an event. Samhain was preparing for his place in the taking of the wolves. It wouldn't show up any more evident to him as he thought about it. Only time would have set in and then people would get picked offed one by one. He surveyed the room.

~ ~ ~

"Scholars please, come together I have words to speak to you." Samhain said as the scholars poured into the sanctuary.

"Does this have anything to do with the guard duty sir." Sicily asked.

"Yeah I have my steps ready to whopping some wolves." Cash said.

"Very well then the enthusiasm is a great touch. I have other matters of questions and the guard duty is now being called surveillance scouting." Samhain said.

"Wait I don't get it." Buckner said.

"Scouting my priest, scouting that will be done by the priest alongside of three other scholars." Samhain said.

"What are we scouting for?" a young scholar asked.

"We my dear, we are scouting for wolves." Samhain said. "We were relieved of our duty as guards yet that will not stop us from guarding the priesthood."

The scholar was shocked at what he said. They were here for a reason and it had to be set in for sure. Samhain had given the next order to the priesthood and they were up for a challenge.

The scholars began taking positions as they all scattered across the front of the priesthood. There wasn't any real form to how they stood. They filed into a crowd. Amongst the priest stood Sicily, Cash and Buckner as they all hand selected three scholars to take with them. They came out with eight groups as some of the priest had to team up. Cash, Sicily, and Buckner all became paired into one group alongside of Rudo.

From there they set out to the borders of the city to interweave through and scout the area for anything that could be taken for wolves. It was set to be a routine check that they would take about every two hours at a time. They would leave a trail after each other creating the perfect circle that was on a constant scout. At least they believed that it would become one. The order was clear and the task was simple, stay on guard.

The first hour was smooth and very complex that they had to weave in and out of some rough terrain of rocks that lay around. Still in the same treat they began making a trail that moved the rough dirt around to show its exact walking premise. It would become the path that they would stay on for the remainder of the process of scouting.

"How long are we going to do this?" Cash said.

"This will be as long as it takes to find the wolves lurking around." Buckner said.

"I know that much but how in the world would four priest keep up with a pack of beastly sized wolves. There has to be a law that governs our own safety!" Cash said.

"Laws are all good in all but Samhain would say it himself. We don't think that the militia would be able to keep up with something as widespread as this is." Sicily said.

"True to think, yet we barely have the tools to do this job alone." Cash said.

"That's coming from a man who knows how to shift into animals or control fire with his bare hands." Sicily said.

"I'm sure you must understand what I am saying?" Cash said.

"Yeah we can get hurt and nobody would be there to help us. We got it Cash." Sicily said.

Cash wasn't moved by what was being said. It had seemed that he had lost some of his courage that once poured out of him before. His attraction to his new girlfriend has taken him backwards a bit that he doesn't wish to relieve. He hopes that nothing would come of this and he hopes for his own sake. The group was trailing the southern part of the border when they heard a loud scream. The shriek had alarmed everyone around that they began running toward the yell.

A young scholar stood helplessly while tangled up in some tree vines and a spider was creeping toward her way. She shrieked morally as the spider creeped, the louder she became the more frightened the others were for her. Upon cornering the young lady a priest had swatted the spider and chopped at the vines that tangled her. To her relief she was free and she let out a loud sigh.

It was easy to see that there was no real danger and that the young lady had been a bore to the scholars. Even Cash rushed to tell the young scholar that she was being a brat. Yet despite his untangling words the scholar had appreciated herself even more that she was afraid of spiders. The groups were full of fight and wanted to know if it would be a change in the appearance of the wolves. Nobody could reason to answer the question, instead all the scholars stood to a silent whelping of thought.

Samhain was within the sanctuary as he was proclaiming what would happen next. He was spending that time in brain storming on how it all would take place and possibly where. Partially it all came back inconclusive and was stretching out Samhain's mind. He was clueless to what to think. He figured that he would have to draw out the wolves somehow and if it was up to him he would figure it out.

The priesthood was continuing onward with the scouting and nothing had reared spec of what to think or how to figure out where the wolves could be. Then it had dawned to Rudo to make a question of something that had bothered him.

"Right after Nattuck bore the eyes of that large wolf, I remembered that it was a woman. She was the woman that jumped to the stage to impact her crew of individuals. The worst thing about it was that she did it all within a shrill moment." Rudo said.

"Not really?" Buckner said.

"Yes really, something weird going on about these wolves and I am clueless to what that could be." Rudo said.

"Well one thing is for sure and it is the fact that wolves don't have the opportunity to change at will. From what the ancient text say about these things is that they only change during a full moon." Buckner said.

"I just guess that we might have a problem then." Rudo said.

"A huge problem, if they can turn at will then we might as well be looking for anybody within …"Buckner said.

"Central." Sicily said.

"Don't be starting things that you have no business starting." Cash said.

"More like investigating." Buckner said.

"We might need to pull more evidence on this." Cash said.

"Remember we did Cash. Last year in Idel near Natu's bridge we met that strange man." Sicily said.

"I remember, that was when he tried to take you from us." Cash said.

Things were different for sure and the newly renowned priest was sure of that and they only wanted to put a touch to how things were changing. The facts that brought the new lead had changed their perspective on what to think about. They weren't too far into the clear just yet. It was easy to say who isn't an average person of central yet to who could tell. That's when it hit them.

Genesis was within the church when the group of priest had entered in. The stir of commotion that they carried had set them afar from the strict level of concentration that Genesis was on. It was all tying in and they needed a favor form him.

~~~

Sicily stood staring out of her bedroom window when Cash had walked in on her. It would appear that he wanted to comfort whatever that was missing from her regular stride of stepping over to his room before sleep time. Neither one had casted a word to each other and the moment was taking in time.

"I guess I missed you, why haven't you come to see me?" Cash said.
~~~

Sicily was still tied to the window and didn't resort to responding. Something had captured her mind and was throwing her off. It was as if the very spirits of last year had drawn her to an attraction as she said that she could see the spirits. Cash had heard her clearly and wasn't too sure what it was that he was hearing. This is to the point that they carried the spirits of the politician's family within them still and they carried a draw to other souls.

Cash spent some time trying to figure out what she was talking about and why is this feeling coming on now out of all. She didn't, she couldn't explain it to him as easily as he had wanted to know. It was harder for her to explain it all what it was pecking at Andrea. The disturbance was keeping Cash on high alert and Joe felt the disturbance. The spirits that lived by with them can tell something was very different.

~ ~ ~

The night was drawing late and Buckner was up late talking with priestess Elee. It would seem that he was trying to spend time with his family when the priestess had separated his thoughts.

"This whole time I had thought that things were going good, a bit too well but it's almost as if nothing is adding up. When it comes to us, I'm happy." Elee said.

"Sweetie I'm happy too." Buckner said.

"Not really now? Yet something is still telling me that we shouldn't be what we are. If I spent any real time trying to figure this out then maybe I wouldn't be having this dilemma right now."

Elee said.

"Dilemma, what dilemma, everything is fine…" Buckner said.

"What is fine Buckner, look at us." Elee said.

Buckner had blacked out. He didn't understand why the priestess was upset yet he knew what it related towards.

"Yes and look at us, you had my child and things are just starting to turn around for us." Buckner said.

"Turn around, why not try to turn around whatever is happening to your son if you think things is pretty fine!" Priestess Elee said.

Buckner had been put into a position that he knew he couldn't turn away from. It was only as if the priestess was making a statement toward how she had felt and it was making a lot of sense. Sense that Buckner didn't want to hear when it comes to his own child. He was fast into thought on how time would be spent and what type of activities that they would spill into. The whole accordance was being out written and taken for less.

He drew into spending more time with his son who was now floating on his own will. Sure the child was different yet it was Buckner who felt that his life could make a difference in a life like what they have. He would be unjustly in saying that the child couldn't be any more important than anyone else. Though that wasn't the way that Buckner was as a person. Something was coming and he knew that things could play out pretty well if he believed in his son. He was drawing into his own ideas of what to think and it was becoming unhealthy to him that he had to fight so hard.

The two continued onward in spending time with one another and the time was moving forward as usual. Buckner spent the time trying to keep his child from floating to the ceiling as he cooed and laughed. The well grown child was making a mark on what he wanted and it was play time. Buckner had spent close to four hours with him and he was drawing into being tired and weak due to being up all morning. Since his son's birth it was the routine that he had for the last ten months and it was taking its toll.

Buckner heeded to the priestess into taking the child so that he may leave to go to sleep and she did. She knows very well how he felt about the child and that he would do anything to keep him safe and calm yet it was taking a lot out of him to stay up any later. He had to be up early in the morning and continue onward with the city watch and he had to take his post. She felt positive that she was doing the right thing by keeping the child. At least she felt that way about how she sees Buckner's eyes light up when he gets the chance to see them together.

He took a slow stroll back to the sleeping quarters and was pretty tired as he wobbled as he walked. He was deprived of sleep and he begged of it with his body movement. The slow stroll was giving him a feel of imaginative distilment as he began seeing things that couldn't be on any average day. The hall sparkled with a blue light that made the hallway shimmer in the dim darkness. People had begun to appear as he walked right up to them.

"Hush please be quiet, we don't want to wake any of the sleeping people here." A voice cried out.

"I can hear you!" Buckner said.

"Aagh." The voice cried back.

"Wait mistress, he can see us." Another voice cried out.

A crowd of oohs came afterward and the shimmering blue light had got brighter. Of course he could see them, not that it had mattered that they were dead souls.

"My-gosh who in the world are you? How can you see us?" The voice said.

"Well who I am may not be all that important as to who knows I might fulfill your thoughts." Buckner said.

Buckner withdrew the spirit that had settled within him as he flaunted his level of understanding. It was a first time for the spirits to see another spirit that was attached to a human soul.

"Isn't that just a sight to see." A voice said.

"Please, man of powerful understanding we are here to release the spirits that are locked here." A spirit said.

"Why, they bid no one any harm and they are pretty settled." Buckner said.

"Settled," The spirits meddled. "We are here because we have unfinished business in this world."

"Is that right?" Buckner questioned.

"Sure it is, we are spirits living in this desolate plain that is between life. Others had left before us and we saw them all go to heaven and God had told us to join together and finish a special task that he had left for us." The spirit said.

"What is the special task that he wants you to complete? I'm sure he wouldn't leave you hanging and not tell you what it was." Buckner said.

"Well, of course he did. The only thing is that we can't come together to get it all started. We have to do this or all will be lost for all of our loved ones." The spirit said.

"I do hope that you all get to go back home, I would hate it if something like that had happened to me or even one of my loved ones." Buckner said.

"Just be lucky that it isn't, now we got some business to get to." The spirit called out.

The door to the basement was closed and none of the spirits could grab hold of the door knob. Buckner had almost laughed when he noticed them yet he didn't budge in doing so. He knew that these spirits would have a wordld of hurt ahead of them before they would come to finishing their task. So Buckner decided to give them a hand of help in opening the door when Alona had approached them.

"Hey, it's good to see everyone. I felt you all for some time now and I didn't think I would get this close to anyone." Alona said.

"We came looking for all of the lost spirits of Central and now we are almost complete in doing so. I feel the presence of more spirits in the politician's mansions." The spirit called out.

"How all of these spirits are getting around out here. I mean you think there is more at the politician's mansion huh." Alona said.

"It would seem that there is more than what meets the eye." Buckner states.

"And how are you dad?" Alona said.

The spirit of Joe came from Buckner and gave a brief look at Alona. It has been a while since he spoke to her yet he never left the side of Buckner. Ever since they had merged he never came to the thought that he would be missed by his own daughter. He knew something was a fray and yet he still hasn't placed his hands on it yet.

"Hello sweetheart. I am still looking into something right now. I think I almost covered it all." Joe said.

"All of what?" The group of spirits called out.

"I almost found out the mystery of what is contained within

this city." Joe said.

"How close are you to it?" Alona said.

"Very close!" Joe said.

As the group spoke Sicily can be seen walking down the hall as Andrea pours out of her. "You all are here." Andrea said.

"Mom," Alona said, "what are you doing here now."

"I saw the spirits and I figured that they might be up to something so I wanted them to come here and they did." Andrea said.

"Wait mom I'm not getting it. You called for the other spirits to come here?" Alona said.

"No." Joe said. "There here because they have something to do and it might involve us all."

"Wait now I'm confused." Alona said.

"Well don't be confused sweetheart. You are Alona right, the niece of the Politician Jasper right." A spirit called out.

"Of course I am, why would you ask?" Alona said.

"What is it that you know about the Politician?" The spirit called out.

"Not much, I heard that he was a great and noble man who was to be the greatest thing to this community." Alona said.

"That is something that is rhetorical if it would involve being a pet or subject of things that aren't exactly to our likings." The spirit said.

"I don't understand, what is it that you are trying to say?" Alona said.

"We really don't understand as to what has happened or how he is involved yet we were told that he holds the key to our return to the afterlife." The spirit said.

"He is the key to our return to the afterlife. I understand what you are saying it is just … I've been here for almost ten, twelve years and I always thought that this was the afterlife." Alona said.

"No sweetie, heaven is where we are getting prepared for. Heaven is where we belong and that is where they are trying to go." The spirit said.

"So we are all locked out of heaven then?" Alona ask.

"Yes but we are on our way home soon enough sweetie, soon enough." The spirit replied.

Between the commotions nobody knew what was to take place yet they knew that it involved Jasper. It would be sinister to give a firsthand statement to say that they had always figured his place yet they knew none. Buckner tried to brainstorm how in the world Jasper was involved but couldn't figure it through his complex of thoughts. He didn't mind overthinking as much as he was trying to get prepared to go to sleep. The restlessness was settling in and he had much less to offer any real attention to any detail.

"Sicily I'm going to prepare for bed, can you handle this?" Buckner asked.

Sicily gave in and told him that it would be best for him to sleep and that he should expect them all to be gone for the nights to come. Buckner thanked her heavily and went off to bed. Sicily was stuck in conversation with the spirits as she reasoned with Andrea to stay with her for the time to come when Genesis had walked into the mix.

"Priestess Sicily, whom are you talking to?" Genesis asked.

The priestess was stuck to give a divine answer that would encourage anything that wasn't what it was yet she tried and the words haven't snuck past the priest. He for shadowed divinity as Samhain had put it and it was his place to seek the truths of the world. Yet it was certain that he was incapable of seeing the spirits that lurked within the city walls. In true reality nobody could accept those who bore the most of faith and truly believed it. The astonishment had crashed over Sicily with a devastating blow, to who was Genesis anyway.

"I would have to say that I've spent way too much time staying up and that I just might be a bit too tired for the moment." Sicily said.

"That is quite fine and all and you should feel happy to be

getting some rest for once." Genesis said.

"Yes I am, I will escort myself out if you don't mind and with a since of prayer could you deliver my friends and Andrea to me?" Sicily said.

"Sure can, Dear father let us take the time to give you thanks for the peace and harmony that you have bestowed to us for the moment and we hope for more times like this in this depressing times. To Andrea and her friends of Sicily I ask that you would deliver them to her and that you keep watch over them as we awake in a frame of life that isn't even handed for most people in this city…" Genesis said.

"Yes and that is so helpful that I will be leaving now." Sicily said.

Andrea had noticed what was going on and told the spirits to take a moment to follow her to the priestess room and they should have a way out of the sanctuary. It was a timid trick, yet it will work out well. The priestess felt proud and yet afraid of what was to come.

~ ~ ~

It was a couple of days until the night of the politician and family ties couldn't have been any stronger. Lurking behind the scene of things a woman began to cry within the middle of the night. She had lost her husband just a year ago at the politicians party to the crazed wolves and it was just this morning when she had last seen her two beautiful children. The woman was lost and tormented with grief that she cried to anyone who would listen.

"Please, please help me! I've lost my children. Anyone please help me search for my children." The woman cried.

Throughout the night the woman walked and begged for her justly help and no one was there to consider her asking. Not even the night guards would take to her claim that she begged and begged so much for. The woman had sat at a fountain that sat in the middle of the town court as she wiped and screamed for help. The screams that carried a tune had stretched throughout the night sky from the house of Jasper all the way to the sanctuary.

Jasper stood from his window staring outward into the courtyard toward the woman. He watched her cry for hours before he finally turned away. It was time that Jasper had made a move again since the coming of his annual political party that was just a week away. The peace of Central had been taken away and it was up to him the people's champion. It would've been fair to say that Jasper hadn't known what he was going to do yet it involves doing some hard work.

He called for a special meeting amongst his peers and he began speaking in a high end resolution. He tried to define what the end was looking like for his team and that it could happen at any time.